Private Affairs

By Anie Michaels

Edited by

Hot Tree Editing

Any trademarks, service marks, product names or named features are assumed to be the property of their respective owners, and are used only for reference. There is no implied endorsement if we used one of those terms.

This is a work of fiction. Names, characters,

Chapter One

Thwap.

That was the noise which brought me out of my fuzzy, morning fog. Putting my coffee mug down, I looked at the granite countertop to see the envelope that had just been tossed there. I looked around to see if he was anywhere near me still, but all I caught was his back as he walked out of the front door. I sighed and glanced at the rectangle staring back up at me. My name was scrawled across the front, hastily written, slanted and sloppy.

Lena

I was hoping we could just ignore the significance of this day. Hoping we could just continue to live in comfortable silence and not draw any more attention to the marriage that was so completely and utterly failing.

Every day I woke up wondering which emotion would rule me. Would I be sad? Sad that the man I'd once loved was more like a roommate than a partner? Would I be angry? Angry he'd physically and emotionally abandoned me, both of which he'd vowed never to do? Would this be the day I was happy? Happy that I wasn't tied emotionally any longer to a man who obviously couldn't fulfill his obligations as my husband? Most days I managed to make the rounds and visit every emotion humanly possible, slowly fading from one to the next.

Today, unusually, I was filled with sorrow. Reminded by the greeting card sitting on my counter, today I grieved the loss of my marriage. For seven years we'd been married, and if I was really being honest with myself, we'd only been happy for about two of those.

I picked up the envelope and slid my finger beneath the lip, trying to open it without tearing the paper. I pulled the card out and read the sentiments pre-printed inside. None of the words meant anything to me; didn't evoke any emotion, because they were empty. He bought this card because he thought he had to. He hadn't even written anything on the inside. No personal note, no words to make me believe or hope that perhaps there was still something of our marriage to salvage. Nothing. I put the card down and exhaled slowly.

Seven years ago I married my college boyfriend and I remembered being replete with love and excitement. I met Derrek during my sophomore year at a frat party. I hadn't been a part of the Greek system and felt overwhelmingly out of place, having been dragged there by my roommate, Samantha. I stood in the corner of the room, holding up a wall, slowly sipping on some sugary, fruity drink in a red cup.

While I looked around the room, trying not to seem as uncomfortable as I felt, I noticed a guy staring at me. Our gazes locked and I was immediately stunned by the deep blue of his eyes. Being caught off-guard by their beauty, I hadn't noticed them coming closer, or who they belonged to. When they were suddenly right in front of me, returning my gaze, I was forced to acknowledge the person they were attached to. Not surprisingly, the most beautiful eyes I'd ever seen belonged to the most beautiful man I had ever encountered. How convenient.

He was smiling, his full lips sliding over his white teeth, as he leaned against the wall next to me.

"I've never seen you here before," he said, still smiling. His voice was deep and playful. Nothing about him was off-putting. Everything about him screamed perfection.

That should have been my first indication to run the other way. Instead, I leaned in a little closer.

"That's probably because I've never been here before," I answered, talking loudly to be heard over the music and other party noises.

"Well, welcome then."

"Thanks."

He reached his hand out to me. "My name's Derrek. It's nice to meet you."

"Lena," I said, taking his hand. His grip was firm, but not overpowering. He held on to my hand longer than necessary, his smile never wavering as he slowly shook it. When he finally dropped my hand, it had immediately felt colder and a little empty.

He spent the rest of the evening chatting with me. He was very attentive, never paying attention to any other girls, only saying a few words to his friends who occasionally passed by. He seemed to be fully interested in spending the night talking to me, which was more flattering than I ever expected. At one point, the music and laughter in the house made it difficult to hear each other, so he'd asked if I wanted to go for a walk. My stomach fluttered at the thought of spending time with him completely alone, but something about him, which I couldn't exactly pinpoint, made me comfortable.

"Let me go and tell my friend I'm leaving," I said, smiling at the thought of leaving with him.

"Great. I'll meet you out front when you're ready."

Samantha had given me the obligatory best friend lecture about going for walks in the dark with strangers, and she'd been right; I was about to break every rule we college girls had been warned against. But I had a cell phone with a good battery charge and I also had pepper spray on my keychain. I was confident I would be fine.

And it turned out that I would be fine – for a while.

We walked around campus all night, continuing our conversation from the party and talking about so much more. By the time the sun came up, we were holding hands and strolling toward my dorm. We walked up the concrete stairs and stopped by the door. Both of us made some comment about how much fun we'd had, and I thought my heart would melt when he leaned in and kissed my cheek.

After that night we were inseparable. We found ourselves in an instant relationship. It had seemed so natural, and everything about it was perfect. We had similar backgrounds and our lives almost seemed to mirror each other's.

Both of our fathers had started their businesses from the ground up, and both had become immensely successful CEOs, so both Derrek and I were familiar with the lifestyle of the upper class. We'd played different roles, but they complemented each other. Derrek was being groomed to one day take over his father's role in the company, while I was expected be a wife to someone just like him. I hadn't planned on becoming someone's arm candy – I would have my own life and my own career – but I was expected to make a good match for someone important one day. My parents would not have been happy if I up and married a starving artist. I was expected to marry someone who would fit nicely into the life my parents had made for me, and honestly, up until a few years after I was married, I had no problem with that notion.

But there I was, seven years into my marriage, and I was anything but happy.

I pulled myself out of the memory of meeting Derrek and slowly walked to the garbage, dropping the anniversary card on top of all the other trash inside. I didn't understand why he'd given it to me, other than perhaps he was trying to stave off an argument. But we hadn't argued in forever. To argue, one had to communicate, even if it was angry, loud, harsh communication. The most we said to each other over the past few weeks had been stilted, forced conversations pertaining to upholding our appearances. We still went to functions together, still played the part of a happily married couple, but when we came home, we separated.

I always found myself alone in our king-sized bed, and he always found himself asleep on the pull-out couch in his office. We could go days without seeing each other if we tried, and sometimes I did try. I tried to pretend as if he wasn't there, as if I wasn't trapped in some loveless marriage any longer, but even that was depressing. If I wasn't married to Derrek, I was living an empty life in an even emptier house.

Something needed to change, and in that moment, I decided, perhaps, it had to be me.

I had loved him once, a long time ago, when careers and expectations hadn't been on our radar. When we'd been young and, in many ways, free. When love hadn't been a means to fulfill the wishes of our parents, but had been born out of our inability to stay away from one another. Truth be told, I still loved him; loved the idea of him, of us. But that need for him had disappeared. I wanted it back – desperately.

I made the decision in that moment to try to fix us. To do whatever was needed to make my marriage work again, and not just be a roommate to my husband. I wanted to be his wife again.

Chapter Two

When I heard the front door open that evening, it signaled Derrek was home from work and also signaled the beginning of my attempt to win my husband back. My heart nearly stopped and I had to talk myself down from the proverbial ledge. I was nervous to be alone with my own husband, apprehensive about putting myself in the line of fire. But something needed to change;

something had to give. I'd been ambitious my whole life – a doer. If I saw a problem at my job, I fixed it. In all other aspects of life, if something needed attention, I focused until I was the victor. I was determined to make my marriage work and not be miserable for the rest of my life.

"Derrek, is that you?" I heard his footsteps falter. He'd been making a hasty retreat to his office, as he did most evenings upon arriving home. My question caught him off guard.

"Yes. It's me."

"Would you come to the dining room, please?" There were a few seconds of silence, and then I heard footfalls coming closer. When he entered the room I tried not to be discouraged by the expressions that crossed his face. At first, I saw annoyance, more than likely that I'd asked something of him. Then the annoyance gave way to surprise, which eventually turned back into annoyance. I watched as his gaze floated over to the table, taking in the lit candles, the use of our wedding china, the beautiful meal I'd made, and the bottle of expensive wine airing.

"Lena, what is all this?" he asked, as his hand made a sharp jab toward the table and then fell to his side.

"This is the anniversary dinner I made for us," I said with a shaky smile, trying so hard not to sound desperate or false. I attempted to sound like this was something he should have been expecting – his loving wife preparing a delicious meal to celebrate seven years of marriage.

"Lena…" he said, with defeat heavy in his voice. I could fill in the blanks, say the words he was thinking; I'd thought them for so long, too. *This is ridiculous. I don't know what you expect from me. What are we doing? How long can we keep this up without ruining our lives?* I knew what was running through his mind, but I needed to stop him from uttering the words, because once we said them, once they were out in the open, we could never cover them up again.

"Please, Derrek, sit down. I made your favorite. Beef roast. Just sit." I was begging my husband to have a meal with me.

He sighed heavily, but set his briefcase on the ground near the entryway and sat down at the head of the table. I smiled to myself because this was the first hurdle, and we'd already jumped it and landed on the other side unscathed. I walked to his chair, hoping to catch his eyes admiring me in the dress I bought to impress him.

I was barely thirty, never had children, and worked very hard to maintain my body. My dress was black, tight, and just a little short. I watched his eyes, hoping they'd roam over me, hoping that seeing him appreciate my form would spark some sort of fire within me.

He never looked at me. He was focused on his plate.

"Did you have a good day at work?" I asked innocently, like it was a question I asked him every evening.

"I suppose. I was busy. Lots of meetings."

"Oh, well, hopefully you'll be able to relax tonight."

I picked up the platter of roast and carried it to him, stood there as he picked up the fork and started serving himself. I took him in, looked over his profile. His hair looked a little messy, which was abnormal for him. He was usually put together, always immaculately pristine. His hard day of work must have stressed him out more than he let on. It looked as if he'd run his hands through his hair all day, undoing any styling he'd invested in this morning before he left the house.

My eyes wandered still lower, along the thickness of his neck. The muscles that ran from his chin down to his shoulders flexed as his jaw clenched. He looked nervous, and I saw his pulse beating rapidly along his throat.

"Are you feeling all right?" I asked, genuinely concerned.

"I'm fine, Lena. Let's just get on with this." I was startled by his rudeness. He was often cold toward me, removed and stiff, but never rude.

I was turning away from him, moving to grab the bowl of roasted potatoes, when my eye spotted something down inside the collar of his shirt. Before I could stop it, my finger involuntarily moved to his collar and pushed it aside gently and I saw more of what had caught my eye to begin with.

"Did you hurt yourself?" I asked, and at the same time, he swatted my hand away from his neck.

"No, I didn't hurt myself. Lena, this is ridiculous. I have things to do."

My mind swirled with different thoughts and feelings as I tried to process everything that was happening. One thing became abundantly clear in that moment: he was hiding something from me. What I had first spotted and assumed was a bruise along his collarbone, I realized, like a bucket of cold water dumped on me unexpectedly, was a hickey.

He stood abruptly, the sound of the chair legs scraping against the travertine tile floors sending shivers down my spine, like nails on a chalkboard. I'd always hated those tile floors.

"Where are you going?" I asked hurriedly, trying to catch him before he made it all the way out of the room. Although, I could guess where he was headed – his office. If he was home and awake, he was usually hiding in there. He knew I had no business being in there, and so that was how he escaped me.

"Like I said, I have things to do." He continued out of the room and I set the platter down, following him.

"What could be more important than having a meal with your wife on your anniversary?" I shouted at him as I followed him through the house, my voice echoing off the walls. I heard him sigh loudly again, but he still walked away from me.

"Lena, don't do this." He had entered his office and sat down at the big chair behind his desk.

"Don't do what? Make you dinner? Ask to spend time with you? Why can't we *try* to be normal or maybe even happy, just for one night? We used to be happy, Derrek. We used to be in love and happy. I just wanted to try and get a little happiness back tonight."

He was silent for a moment, shuffling papers around on his desk, avoiding my eyes. He moved those papers around, stacking them on one corner of his desk, and then moved them to another corner. He tapped on his keyboard, stared at the screen of his computer like the answers to all the world's problems could be found there. One thing he wouldn't look at was me.

"You can't ignore me, Derrek. I'm your wife."

"I'm aware of that fact," he mumbled, sounding angry.

"What was that mark I saw under your shirt collar, Derrek?"

"I don't know what you're talking about."

"I think you do."

"Lena, please…" He pinched the bridge of his nose. "I don't understand what's gotten into you."

"I spent all day trying to think of how I could surprise you for our anniversary, trying to think of ways to get back that spark we use to have between us, and you come home with a hickey under your shirt."

"You're being ridiculous," he said under his breath.

"Am I?"

"Yes."

"Then take off your shirt."

He paused, obviously not expecting me to say those words. I hadn't asked him to take off any piece of clothing in months. Perhaps even over a year. I'd have to really think about it to come up with a solid answer.

"Lena, please, let's stop deluding ourselves," he finally replied, finally lifted his eyes to look me straight in mine.

"I don't think I'm deluding myself. I know what I saw."

"Our marriage, the part of our relationship where we have meals together or spend time alone together, is over. It's been over for a long time now. You know it. I know it. I'm content with the way things are now."

"What do you mean, 'it's over'?" I gasped.

"We haven't behaved like a married couple for years now, Lena. Out in the public eye, we continue to hold up the image of our marriage, but here – in this house – our marriage fell apart long ago."

I agreed with him, knew what he was saying to be true, but I didn't think it was a lost cause, didn't think it was doomed. He sounded like it was dead and gone. I just felt like it needed some work – could be resuscitated.

"So let's fix it," I cried.

"We can't. It's too late."

"So, what? You want a divorce? You're going to leave me?" The image of that hickey flashed into my mind. "You're having an affair?"

"I am *not* having an affair." His voice was cold and stone-like. His affirmation was almost like a gust of chilling wind; it hit me hard and made me shiver. "I am, however, going back to the office. It's abundantly clear I won't be able to get any work done here tonight."

I watched as he stood again and walked right past me, walking back toward the dining room. He retrieved his briefcase and walked toward the front door. When I heard it open and then subsequently slam shut, I felt the loud sounds vibrate through me, and felt a little crack form in the façade I'd been wearing for what seemed like forever. It seemed as if, in one thirty minute window, we'd moved from pretending our marriage was fine to acknowledging its failure, but I was still left wallowing in confusion.

I walked slowly to the dining room, mindlessly clearing the table, just going through the motions while my mind reeled.

What were we to do? Just continue on this path of sharing a house but sharing nothing besides? My hands dipped in and out of the warm, soapy water, washing the dishes, rinsing them, and then setting them on the rack to dry. We had a dishwasher, but washing them by hand calmed me.

I didn't want a marriage of convenience, but from his words, it seemed like Derrek had thrown in the towel and wanted nothing to do with me. Well, aside from a companion to accompany him to work functions and parties. He wanted to hold up the appearance of our marriage, but drop the charade at the door.

I saw a tear drop into the dishwater. Not realizing I was crying, the tear caught me off guard. Once I saw the first one fall, however, the rest were not far behind.

This was not where I wanted to be, wasn't how I envisioned my life to be at twenty-nine. When I married Derrek, I was sure we'd be happy forever. Sure, I suspected we'd have difficult times, trying times, but I thought we'd work together to get past them.

I never would have imagined that one day Derrek would tell me our marriage was over, that the real part – the loving part – had been lost.

Then there was the hickey he denied.

Of everything that happened, the hickey was the least of my worries. Well, it would have been if he'd owned up to it. We couldn't work past a problem if he didn't admit to it, and I would gladly, at this point, look past any transgressions on his part if he'd just agree to be my husband again.

I cried because he didn't want me and I cried because I still wanted him. I wanted my marriage. I wanted the future I'd signed up for so many years ago, and I didn't think it was fair that someone else could make those decisions for me. Didn't I get a say in how our future played out?

My hand slammed down on the counter, suds spraying out around my wet hand.

"Shit," I cried through a whisper. Perhaps I shouldn't have ambushed him with this dinner. Perhaps I should have approached him on a different night, some other time when the pressure wasn't so high. I should have let our anniversary pass by and tried to talk to him when he was more relaxed and not so obviously stressed. All those thoughts just made me cry harder. I never wanted to have to walk on eggshells around my husband. I also cried harder because I could remember a time when I didn't have to, when I could go to him with any problem I was having or any emotion I was feeling.

Once the dishes were clean and the dining room was put back in order, I ambled up the stairs and readied myself for bed, not expecting to see Derrek for the rest of the evening. And I was right. He never came home that night.

Chapter Three

I woke to the sound of my phone buzzing against the wood of my bedside table. I hadn't set an alarm and wasn't expecting to be woken up, so I startled a bit. The buzzing stopped, and before I could reach over to see what had caused it, I must have fallen asleep again because I was awoken by the buzzing a second time. This time, however, the damage was done and I was awake. A groan escaped me as I rolled over to see who was trying to contact me. I pressed the button on the phone to light up the screen and saw two text messages from Samantha.

Hey, woman. How did the surprise anniversary dinner go?

You're either still asleep because you're exhausted from all the sex you and your husband had last night, or because you cried yourself to sleep. Either way, we need to talk. Text me back.

I sighed at her intuitive mind. Couldn't I have just been asleep because I was sleeping? Maybe I went for a run last night and was exhausted from that. I wasn't really surprised that she'd clued in to what had really happened, but I was more upset that now I was probably going to have to talk to her about it. Talking about it to someone else made it real. I wasn't trying to delude myself into thinking I had a perfect marriage, but admitting to my best friend that last night had put some sort of nail in my marriage coffin would be the most real and heartbreaking conversation I might ever have. It occurred to me I would have this real and heartbreaking conversation with my best friend and not my husband, and that, perhaps, was the most depressing and telling thought of all.

I pressed the buttons on my phone to send a message back to her.

Same time, same place?

It only took a few seconds for her to respond.

See you there.

Years ago, Samantha and I had found a tiny little coffee shop equidistant between our houses, and we'd started meeting there for coffee weekly, or whenever one of us called upon the other. It was nice, all those years, to have something steady and reliable to hang on to – something to look forward to. Sometimes, we didn't have anything new or exciting to talk about and we just reminisced, laughing about things that happened in college or since. Other times, I held her hand as she told me about her break-ups, or we listened to each other's work problems, trying to ease the anxiety of navigating the working world as young and independent women.

I met Samantha when we'd been assigned as dorm roommates our freshman year of college. She and I couldn't have been any more different. She was outgoing, brave, and brought energy with her wherever she went. Her vitality was contagious, and as soon as we met, I felt the fever she carried with her for life. I had spent my entire life protected from the adventurous spirit she exuded, and when I got a taste of it, I grabbed ahold of her and never let her get away. She taught me how to let go, how to feel free even if I really wasn't. When I was with her, I could sometimes pretend I didn't have my father to answer to, or a life waiting for me that I wasn't sure I wanted to live.

When I was twenty-four, my father passed away suddenly, and even though I was internally conflicted over my feelings toward his death, she was there for me every step of the way. I didn't have to explain to her that I was devastated my father was dead, but relieved that I no longer had to worry about living up to his standards for me. His death saddened and freed me all in the same moment. She knew it, understood, and never judged me. Not once.

Samantha had spent many hours listening to me talk about my marriage. She knew everything about it – the good and the bad. She also had very strong feelings about it.

She hated Derrek.

It hadn't always been that way; he hadn't always been the spawn of Satan in her eyes. All through college, Derrek and Sam got along really well. We spent countless Saturday nights at his frat house and the two of them never had one argument. She was my maid of honor in our wedding. She was so happy for us – so supportive. However, when the marriage began to change, began to fall into the dark place it seemed to reside in now, she always questioned why I stayed with him.

I hated complaining to her about him or our relationship, because it did nothing but further tarnish him in her eyes, but I had no one else to turn to. In my family, we didn't talk about problems. It was understood that you were to always keep up appearances. If you had an issue, you resolved it quietly. You didn't bring attention to it. You swept it under the rug.

It was comforting to walk in to our usual coffee shop and see her sitting at a table waiting for me. I went straight for her. She stood when she saw me and opened her arms for me without question, knowing I'd be here with bad news instead of good.

"What happened, Lena?"

I let myself take the comfort from her, allowed her arms to pull out some of my anxiety. I sighed into her shoulder, trying to keep the tears at bay. I didn't want to cry anymore.

"I don't know, Sam." I pulled away and sat in the chair opposite her, giving a sad smile to the cup waiting for me. If Sam made it to the coffee shop first, she always bought my drink, and vice versa. "Thank you for the coffee." She smiled at me, but said nothing. "I made the dinner, put on the dress, and was all ready for him when he came home from work." I dove right into the story. I knew Sam wasn't going to stand for pleasantries and chit chat.

"Did he appreciate it?" she asked, not even blinking.

"No. Actually, he seemed put out by it. Like having dinner with me was an inconvenience to his evening schedule."

"That bastard."

"It gets worse."

"I'm not surprised." She raised her eyebrows, waiting for me to continue.

"When I mentioned I wanted to work on our marriage, that I wanted to get back to the happy couple we had been when we got married, he basically told me our marriage was over and that I should get used to the status quo. He said that our marriage fell apart a long time ago and that it was too late to fix it." Samantha said nothing, but I could tell she was holding her rage inside for my benefit. She knew what I had been hoping for, knew I wanted my husband back. So, out of love for me, she was reining in all the expletives I knew she wanted to unleash, because she knew it wouldn't help me, wouldn't make me feel any better. I loved her even more for it.

I looked down at my coffee cup, slowly twisting it around and around, watching it circle in my fingers, while I continued.

"He wants to hold up the façade of our marriage, you know, still make appearances together in public, but pretty much indicated he was done with me in private." My voice faltered on the last few words, my throat constricting with that painful pinch that was always followed by tears, aching. But I pushed it back. I wouldn't cry any more. "He only wants to be my husband when other people can see us."

Sam was quiet for a few moments more, and then she adjusted in her seat and tilted her head to the side. "Why would any man want to continue a marriage without the *benefits* of marriage? I mean, let's be real. He's a man. I can understand him wanting to stay in the marriage if you were going to try and fix it and work on the intimacy, or I can understand him cutting his losses and wanting out in order to find that intimacy in other places. But what hot-blooded man chooses to stay in a sexless marriage and wants it to remain that way?"

I didn't look up at her and I didn't say anything, afraid to tell her what I'd seen under his shirt collar. Being a terrible husband, being absent and emotionally unavailable, was bad enough. If I told her what I saw, she'd likely be unstoppable in her rage and find him to take her anger out on him. She would also try to pressure me into leaving him, and I knew I couldn't do that. I also knew she'd never be able to understand why. The mistake I'd made before our marriage had even begun would keep me tethered to him.

I sighed loudly and shook my head. "I couldn't fathom the thoughts running through his mind. Perhaps in a few days I can try to talk to him again. Maybe I just caught him at a bad time."

"Your wedding anniversary was a bad time for him to talk to you?" she asked snidely. I didn't take offense. I knew she wasn't angry with me.

"He's stressed at work," I mumbled.

"Don't make excuses for him, Lena."

"Sorry."

"Don't apologize either!"

"What do you want from me?"

"I want you to take a stand! Don't let him walk all over you and don't let him make all the decisions! It's your marriage, too, Lena. It's your life just as much as it is his."

I heard her words, felt them sink into me, and then I felt them fall away. I was conflicted. Before I could stop them, the words were falling out of my mouth. "I think he's cheating on me," I whispered.

Sam didn't blink, didn't breathe. She just looked at me as she formulated her thoughts. "Why do you think that?"

"Last night, when he came home, I saw something inside his shirt near his collar. At first, stupidly, I thought it was a bruise. But I eventually realized it was *not* a bruise. It was a hickey."

"Did you ask him about it?"

"I tried, but he changed the subject and left."

"Hmm. Suspicious," she said, warily. I nodded. We were both quiet for a few minutes. I replayed the whole evening in my mind, running through each and every thing I could have done differently. But no decisions I'd made or words I could have said differently changed the fact that he'd come home with that mark on him. A mark another woman had put on him.

"Why don't you leave him, honey?" Sam's words were a quiet whisper, as if her voice could have scared me away. She was treading lightly, not wanting me to turn away from the direction the conversation was heading.

"I can't," I whispered, just as quietly.

"Yes," she said, placing her hand over mine. "You can." I shook my head slightly, feeling my hair sway back and forth over my ears.

"No," I whispered again. I tipped my head up to look her in the eyes again. "I can't, Sam. Really. It's complicated."

"How can I help?"

I shrugged. My next words were drowning in tears, choked out on sobs. "I don't know." *I don't know.* Those three words were the answer to a lot of questions I had running through my mind. Was there any hope left for my marriage? Would I spend the rest of my life tied to a man who didn't want to be with me? Would I feel this lonely forever? Would I go the rest of my life without feeling a man's hands on me again? My head fell into my hands as I tried to cry discreetly in the coffee shop. I heard Sam move and then heard her next to me before I felt her arms come around me. I leaned into her and let the tears come, but stifled the sobs, tried to hold at least those in.

"What are you going to do?" Sam finally asked after I'd calmed down a little.

"Well," I said, wiping my eyes. "I guess I'm going to find out if he's really cheating on me."

"The hickey isn't enough proof for you?"

I shook my head again. "Listen," I started, unsure of how I could explain something to her I'd never explained to anyone. Unsure of how to say the words I'd never uttered to a single soul. "I can't just go on a hunch," I said quietly. "I need actual proof."

"For peace of mind?" she asked.

I nodded. "Sure."

She tilted her head to the side again, her eyebrows narrowing at me. "What's going on, Lena?"

"I'm sorry. I can't go into any more detail than that. All I'm saying is, if anything is going to change, I need actual, physical proof he's cheating. Me spying what I think is a hickey on the inside of his collar isn't going to cut it."

"Well, then," Sam said with resolution in her voice. "We'd better get a rental car, some black turtlenecks and ski masks, and brush up on our stakeout skills."

"What?" I said, half laughing.

Sam had a sneaky smile on her face when she answered me, rubbing her hands together. "We're going to stalk your husband."

Chapter Four

I sat in the passenger seat of a black Toyota Corolla, quietly crunching on Cheetos, my eyes glued to the front doors of my husband's work. Cheetos, in hindsight, might have been a bad snack choice when wearing all black, and I struggled to keep the neon orange cheese powder from making its way into the fibers of my new turtleneck. I heard a giggle and looked over at Sam, sitting in the driver's seat.

"What's so funny?"

She took a bite of the licorice in her hand and waved the red rope between us. "We might be some of the worst stalkers ever."

She wasn't wrong, although, we had gotten most of the basics down. Black car? Check. The cover of night? Check. Black clothes to blend into said cover of night? Check and check. But we also might have indulged and turned our rental car into a snack wagon, using our stakeout as an opportunity and excuse to eat gas station fare, which we never really had a valid reason to buy. But under the guise of our stalker outfits, it seemed fitting to break a few rules, even if they were self-imposed.

It had taken two weeks from our original conversation about my husband's possible affair for me to agree to this crazy idea of Sam's. At first, although it was tempting to see if we could find out what was going on, I wasn't really ready to know. I went home from our coffee shop date and pushed the idea of his affair out of my mind. I had gone back to plan A. If I tried to be the perfect wife, perhaps he would come around and want to be my husband again.

So I baked and cleaned and was waiting to be the doting wife when he came home from work. Only, sometimes he never came home from work, and most of the time, when he did come home, it was so late that I was either crashed on the couch in the living room, or had long given up and was asleep in our bed upstairs. On top of that, he often left for work before the sun came up and I would wake to a house just as empty as it had been when I'd fallen asleep.

I counted eight days in a row in which I didn't once lay eyes on my husband.

I saw proof of him and his presence around the house: a coffee mug in the sink, wet towels in the laundry room, opened mail on the counter. But I never saw him and I hadn't spoken to him since our anniversary.

He wouldn't answer when I called him at work, and I was sent directly to voicemail if I called his cell. After about the first five days of silence from him, I stopped trying to reach him at all.

Finally, I decided to take some sort of action, so I called Sam and told her to greenlight her plan. Three nights later we were sitting in a black rental car, watching the doors to my husband's building, waiting for him to exit so we could follow him. It shouldn't have been fun and it shouldn't have felt like an adventure, but it sort of did. It was impossible not to laugh when trapped in a car with my best friend, especially when she was trying her hardest to keep the mood light, trying to entertain me. I knew what she was doing – trying to keep my mind off the idea that we were, in fact, trying to catch my husband in the act of cheating – and I let her do it. I let her make me laugh so hard I cried. I let her rap along to the radio even though she didn't know all the words and made a horrible rapper. And I let her tell me the horror stories of her most recent travels into the world of dating at twenty-nine.

Suddenly, everything lost its humor as I watched Derrek walk out of the building. Both Sam and I were quiet, watching and waiting. When his car pulled onto the road,

Sam gave me a look, silently asking me if I still wanted to go through with our plan. I nodded. She started the engine and pulled out, only a few cars behind his.

I had never tailed a car before and found it was a delicate balance between staying close enough to follow, but far enough away so that you melted into the background. After a few minutes, it became clear he was not headed to our home. I wasn't surprised at all by this fact, but I was, admittedly, a little saddened. I came out with Sam to find out if he was cheating, but now that we were actually in the midst of possibly finding proof, I realized I might not be ready to deal with the reality proof would bring with it.

"You okay, Lena?"

"Yeah," I said. I took on the role of navigator, keeping my eyes on his car and telling Sam which way to turn or which lane to move into so she could focus on just driving. His car took us more than forty-five minutes away from his work. We were a good distance out of the city, far away from our home, and unfamiliar with the area.

"Where in the world is he going?" I asked, knowing Sam didn't have the answer. I hadn't expected to leave the city. I imagined him pulling up to a corner and propositioning a prostitute, or pulling in to a seedy motel to meet up with some random woman. I had never imagined him leading us to suburbia. The further we got away from the city and closer we got to housing developments, the more nervous I became. My body was clued into what was happening and sending me all kinds of signals to run away. My fight or flight instincts were kicking in, and my body was telling me to fly.

But his car kept driving so we kept following. An hour after he'd left his building we watched as he pulled into the driveway of a house. We stopped down the block and turned off the headlights, watching with suicidal fascination. I wanted to look, but I knew on some unconscious level it was going to hurt. Whatever we saw was going to open me up and rip me to shreds, but I couldn't look away.

He opened his car door and climbed out, stretching up toward the sky, obviously tight from the long drive. He grabbed his briefcase from the backseat and walked toward the two-story, cookie-cutter house. When he was halfway up the path to the house, the door opened and my mouth gaped open as a small child ran toward him.

Derrek dropped his briefcase and crouched down, opening his arms. When the child, a girl if her long hair was any indication, made it to him, he picked her up, hugging her tightly. Then, as if my world couldn't fall apart any more, a woman came out of the house, a smaller child held to her hip. She stood on the front porch, watching Derrek and the little girl, a warm smile on her face.

Derrek picked up his briefcase, never putting the little girl down, and walked toward the door and the woman. When they met, he leaned into her and pressed a kiss to her mouth and lingered there, their kiss obviously deep and heated. Then, he bent down a little and pressed a kiss to the forehead of the small child she held. They all turned and went into the perfect house.

"Holy shit." Sam's voice was quiet and confounded. "Holy," she said louder and turned to me. "Shit."

"Sam, please drive away now," I muttered.

"Holy *shit*!" she said as she put the car in drive and made a U-turn, taking us out of the neighborhood without driving past the house. "What in holy hell did we just see, Lena?"

"I think we just found the answer to our question, Sam. Derrek is definitely cheating on me."

"Yeah, no shit." She looked at me with worried eyes. "Sorry, Lena. That just came out. Are you okay?"

No. No, I wasn't. I was currently longing for the orange, Cheeto-dust-filled laughter I'd had about an hour earlier, before I knew for sure my husband was cheating. Only, he wasn't just cheating. No, what he was doing was so much more than cheating. He had a whole other life – a family – an hour outside the city.

Suddenly, I was questioning my own sanity. Questioning whether I had an accurate or firm grip on reality. I had spent the last seven years of my life married to Derrek, hadn't I? We shared a house and a life and a history, right? How, if what I had seen minutes before was true, if he did in fact have a whole other life, hadn't I noticed? How could I have not realized what was going on around me? How did you keep an entire family hidden?

"I'm so confused," I whispered.

"No fucking shit, Lena. What the hell is going on?" Sam sounded frantic, like her grip on reality was also in question.

"Derrek seems to be leading a double life," I said, sounding astonishingly calmer than I was feeling. "Although, truth be told, in order to be leading a double life, both lives have to be *real* lives. Obviously, he's focusing more on his other life than the one he's leading with me."

"Do you think those were his children?" Sam pondered.

"What other conclusion are we to jump to? What other plausible explanation can there be?"

"Does he have a sister? Could those be his nieces or something?"

"I think I'd rather him be leading a double life than think about him kissing his sister like that. Plus, no, he doesn't have any siblings." I took a deep breath in. I knew he was cheating; there was no other explanation. And I knew why the deception was taken to this level. I felt my stomach bottom out and saliva start to pool in my mouth. "Sam, pull over," I cried, my hand coming to cover my mouth. Luckily, we were still in suburbia, so she was able to veer the car to the curb quickly. I opened the door, stumbled out, and I threw up onto the sidewalk. I retched and heaved until there was nothing left in my stomach, and I immediately regretted the neon orange Cheetos.

"Here," Sam said as I climbed back into the car, handing me a bottle of water left over from our snack attack earlier.

"Thanks." I took a sip.

"You all right?" she asked softly.

"Sam, do me a favor and don't ask me dumb questions. I'm not okay. This is not okay."

"Well, what are we going to do now?"

"Can you please just take me home?"

When we finally made it back to my house Sam was reluctant to leave me there alone, but I made her drive away, needing some time to myself.

"If he comes back tonight and you need someone, call me, Lena. Okay?"

"Sure," I said, unconvincingly. Sam reached across the console and wrapped her arms around my shoulders, hugging me close.

"I'm so sorry, Lena. If I thought we were going to see him, see that, I wouldn't have ever pushed you to do this." Her voice was a quiet whisper, and I could hear the remorse and guilt lacing her words.

"It's not your fault, Sam." She didn't respond, just squeezed me a little harder. "I'll call you tomorrow."

When I entered the house, I pushed the door shut behind me and stood in the foyer, listening to the silence. The darkness wrapped around me, the quiet flooding the black space. I'd lived in this house for six years, but never had it felt this huge, empty, or cold.

I took a deep breath and made my way back to my bedroom, walking the entire way in the dark. I didn't need any light. I knew the hallways well enough, and every once in a while I'd pass a room with windows and the moonlight granted me a little visibility. But I didn't want to see the house. I didn't want to see the pictures hanging on the wall. I didn't want to see the couch in the living room Derrek and I made love on multiple times. I didn't want to see his clothes still hanging in the closet.

I walked back to our bedroom and went to my side of the bed, trying to keep my eyes from wandering to his. I slid my shoes off my feet, leaving them to rest on the floor by my bedside table, then peeled off my ridiculous black outfit, and crawled into bed. The cool sheets felt good on my skin, overheated from the events of the evening, my blood running hot from what I'd seen. I rolled toward the window so I wasn't facing Derrek's side of the bed, and I placed my hands underneath my cheek, and gazed out into the darkness.

I spent the entire night awake, resting in that bed, replaying what I'd seen in my head. At one point, I felt a single tear slide down the side of my face and onto my hands, but I hadn't realized I was crying and it didn't last long.

My feelings fluctuated from being angry with Derrek, to being disappointed in myself. One moment I was mad at him for cheating on me, and the next I was angry with him for not just asking for a divorce before he built a whole new family, a whole new life. I was angry with myself, too, perhaps even more than I was with Derrek.

I'd done this to myself, set myself up for this, made myself a victim.

When the sunlight started streaking through the window, I decided to get out of bed and start my day. I wasn't surprised Derrek hadn't come home. He'd looked like he was pretty settled where he had been. I listened all night for the sounds of him coming into the house, but everything was silent. Most of me was glad he hadn't come home, for I hadn't quite figured out what my plan of action was.

I went into our large closet that resembled more of a dressing room than a closet. I found my favorite jogging outfit, pulled it on, and sat on the bench to lace up my jogging shoes. Standing in front of the vanity, I swiped raven hair back from my face and affixed it in a tight ponytail at the back of my head.

When I left the house, I put the passcode into the security system and shut the door behind me. I stopped on the driveway to stretch a little before I took off. There was a treadmill in the gym inside the house, but I never ran on it. Derrek bought it a few years ago and I thought it was silly. I would much rather run outside than on an endless loop facing a wall. When I felt sufficiently warmed up, I started with a small jog up the street. I had a particular route I liked to take and if I ran the loop twice, it was equal to about four miles.

About halfway into my run, I started to feel the freedom I was searching for, the endorphin rush that catapulted me into a space in my mind where I could think clearly.

Derrek no longer loved me; that thought made itself abundantly clear. Surprisingly, once I'd thought it, I realized I had known it for a while. He tolerated me, at best. And although I didn't know if I was still in love with him, I knew things were far from where they'd started. But with all the new information, I knew my plan to try and resurrect our relationship was no longer an option. I needed a new plan.

So I kept running. I reached the four-mile mark and just kept going, hoping for more of that clarity I sought on my runs. Around mile six I stopped, breaths ragged and panting in and out at a rapid pace, with sweat dripping down my forehead. I was bent over, hands on my knees, thoughts racing through my brain.

I was exactly where I thought I'd safeguarded myself against being. This was what I had thought I was planning against. And he was pushing me out. Well, fuck that and fuck him. My house was just a few blocks up and I sprinted the entire way there. When I made it to the front door, I entered the passcode on the doorknob and after hearing the beep indicating the alarm system had been deactivated, I opened the door and stormed in.

I went straight for his office, my feet loudly stomping down the hallway. When I reached the office, I flung open the door and wasted no time heading to his desk. Pulling open drawers, I swept everything out, throwing all the contents on the floor. Not looking for anything in particular, just looking to make a mess, needing to take my anger out on *something*.

When all the drawers were empty, I moved on to the filing cabinet, finding that tossing papers over my shoulder and up in the air relieved almost as much tension as running. Taking something of his and destroying it was liberating and admittedly, made me feel better.

When I found myself ankle deep in forms and documents, breath heaving, hands shaking, I decided I'd done enough damage. I had visions of myself throwing his desktop out of the bay window behind me, but truth be told, I wasn't normally a destructive person and knew that would be going a little overboard.

I did, however, pull back his plush desk chair, rolling it over piles of papers, hearing the wheels crackling over my husband's hard work, and sat down. I wiggled the mouse to wake up the computer and then opened up a browser and went straight to Google. I typed in the words 'private investigator'. I was flooded with results and went back to narrow down my search. I clicked in the text box again and added the word 'Portland'. I hit enter and new results popped up. I scrolled down the page, my eyes gliding over all the information, and I realized I had no idea what I was looking for. One private investigator was just the same as the next, right? I found one listing that said 'PDX Investigates'. I clicked on the link and was brought to a professional looking webpage that claimed the company was licensed and bonded. I had no clue what that meant, but it sounded official enough to me.

Standing, I then jogged to my bedroom, grabbed my cell phone, then jogged back to the computer and dialed the number.

"PDX Investigates. This is Todd. How can I help you?"

"Uh, hi, Todd. My name is Lena and I'm looking for some help. I need someone to find out some information for me about my husband."

"What kind of information are we talking about?" Todd asked, sounding busy and a little annoyed.

"Well, I'm pretty sure he's cheating on me and I'd like someone to help me find out for sure. I need irrefutable proof."

"Sure. We offer a free consultation, but if you decide to hire us to help, the rate is two hundred dollars an hour with a two thousand dollar retainer. Depending on how complicated your case is, we would either bill you monthly for the balance should you exceed your retainer, or refund you what's left if we wrap it up easily."

"All right, that sounds fine." I had no idea what sounded fine. I had no idea what private investigators charged, but at that point, I didn't really care, either. I just needed to move in a new direction and this was the one that made the most sense. "When is your earliest availability for the consultation?"

"One of our agents has an opening tomorrow afternoon. Does one o'clock work for you?"

"Sure. That will be fine."

"Great. Do you need the address to our offices?"

"No, I've got them right here on the computer."

"Great, we'll see you then."

The line disconnected and I felt my breath leave me suddenly. What had my life come to? Hiring private investigators to spy on my husband? I never imagined that this was where I'd be seven years ago when I told Derrek, "I do" through laughter and smiles. I'd been so excited to marry him that I couldn't even contain myself long enough to make it through the vows. I'd smiled and laughed through the entire ceremony, happiness bubbling over. I was nowhere near smiling and laughing now. But I wasn't crying, so I thought that was a step in the right direction.

I took in a deep breath and, even though I didn't think I should have to, I started picking up all the papers I'd strewn across the room. I bagged them all up and put them in the big trash bin in our garage. I couldn't find it in me to care if he needed them or not, more than likely – since he never really spent time here anymore – he wouldn't even notice they were missing.

The next day, I was just about to leave for my appointment at PDX Investigates when my phone rang, showing an unfamiliar number. It wasn't often I received calls from strange numbers, so I answered with a slow and suspicious, "Hello?"

"Is this Lena Bellows?" As soon as I heard the deep and gravelly voice on the other end of the line, I knew I'd never spoken to this man before. I would remember a voice like his, remember the way just him saying my name made shivers run down my spine. I took note of my reaction, but pressed forward with the conversation.

"Yes, this is she. Who am I speaking with?"

"My name is Preston Reid, and we have an appointment. I'm with PDX Investigates."

"Oh, all right. What can I do for you?"

"I am out working on something for a client and won't be able to make it back to the office in time for our meeting. I was hoping you could meet me for a drink so we could discuss your case."

"Oh, um, I suppose. I don't see why not. Where did you have in mind?"

"There's a martini bar on Third, on the East side, called Bartini."

Clever. "But it will only be one in the afternoon. Will they even be open?"

"I know the owners."

"All right. I'll meet you there." The line went dead and I realized the men who worked for PDX Investigates needed to be taught how to end a phone conversation. Twice I'd been hung up on. I grabbed my purse and headed for the door.

When I walked into Bartini, I noticed the elaborate Moroccan theme apparent throughout. There were many round tables with deep red tablecloths draped over them, candles – although unlit at this hour – and gold accents everywhere. There were throw pillows placed on bench seats, golden chandeliers hanging from the ceiling, and beautiful, lush fabrics in all manner of jewel tones draped the walls in lieu of wallpaper or paint. As I was admiring the décor, a man who worked there led me to a table and told me Mr. Reid would be there any minute. He asked me if I would like a drink and, despite the hour, I told him I'd take a vodka martini, wet, and with an olive.

I pulled out my phone to pass the time and noticed a text message from Derrek.

I have to go out of town for a few days on business. Don't expect me home until Sunday evening.

I stared at the message like it was written in braille. Why in the world, after two and half weeks of not seeing each other or even speaking, really, would he send me this message? My blood began to run a little hot at the thought of him shacking up with his other family all weekend, trying to brush me aside with the cover of a business trip. I didn't even bother answering, but tossed my phone back into my purse as my drink was delivered.

I brought the glass to my lips, closing my eyes as the vodka and vermouth slid over my tongue. It had been a while since I'd indulged in a real drink and in this moment, it couldn't have tasted any better. I picked up the skewer that held one green olive and placed it in my mouth, my teeth gliding the olive off and onto my tongue. In that same moment, I saw the door open and I halted, the skewer paused, trapped between my teeth.

A man walked in and part of me hoped and prayed he was there to see me. The other part, the part that wasn't prepared to deal with the type of masculine beauty he possessed, hoped and prayed he would walk right past me. My breath snagged in my lungs as his eyes met mine and he started toward my table.

Dark hair and dark eyes. Eyes so dark, they could have been chocolate. His chestnut hair was shaved short on the sides, but was longer on the top, just long enough to slide through his fingers when his hand ran through it, as it was now. I watched as his big hand came to his forehead and then moved through locks that looked as though they might feel like silk. He was wearing a black leather jacket that looked soft and worn. Although the jacket fit well enough, it hugged his biceps and the sight of the muscles hidden beneath the supple leather made my stomach flip. He wore a black button-up shirt beneath the amazing jacket, the top two buttons undone, and only part of the hem tucked into his faded blue jeans, ending with black leather shoes to match the jacket.

And he came right for me.

He stalked toward me with his eyes zeroing in on mine. I didn't stand when he stopped next to me, did not move a muscle except the ones in my neck that made it possible for my eyes to remain locked on his. My head tilted up, captivated by him, and I couldn't even find the words to utter a greeting.

"Lena?" he asked, one eyebrow raised. There was that voice again. The voice matched the man: hard, dark, rough. My poor body couldn't handle the combination of all the parts that made up that man, especially when they were coming at me at once, assaulting me. My stomach flipped – bottomed out. My heart pounded and my mouth went dry.

"Yea…yes…that's me," I muttered, right after I pulled the skewer from my teeth, which I'd managed to leave hanging there like an idiot. Still not standing or reaching out my hand to shake his. Just staring. He was the one who broke our eye contact, looking at the chair opposite me before he placed himself in it.

"I'm Preston. Thanks for rearranging your schedule and meeting me here instead," he said, nodding at the waiter who appeared a moment later to take his order. "Scotch. Neat." The waiter gave a nod and disappeared again.

"It was no problem," I said in response, surprised I was able to put together a complete sentence. I had never been affected by a man this way before – not even Derrek. Instantly, but just for one tiny second, I felt guilty for the primal and guttural reaction I was having to this man – I was a married woman, after all. But just as quickly as the guilt came on, it slinked away and left me feeling slightly smug. I could, and would, admire this man as long as he was in front of me. And I would enjoy it too.

"So, tell me. How can I be of service to you?" He placed his forearms on the table, clasped his hands together, leaned forward, aimed his coffee colored eyes at me and waited for my response.

"Well," my voice shook, "I am hoping you can do a little investigating for me. I need someone to catch my husband with whomever he's cheating on me with." I lowered my voice a little when the waiter dropped off his drink. I watched as Preston brought the glass to his lips, only just then noticing how full and lush they were, fascinated as he let the smallest sip of scotch past them. I saw his eyes narrow slightly, guessing the burn of the scotch was coating his throat, but other than the small reaction, he looked like someone who drank straight scotch regularly.

Preston reached into his jacket and pulled out a small notebook and pen. He started scribbling notes on a clean sheet and looked back to me.

"What's your husband's name?"

"Derrek Bellows."

"What makes you think he's cheating on you?"

"Is that relevant?" I put my guard up. I didn't feel like explaining how my husband found me inadequate to the beautiful man sitting across from me. His hand lifted his glass to his mouth again and he took another sip.

"The way I see it," he stated, not looking me in the eye, but looking at his glass. "You called *me*. You need *my* help. I don't care why your husband is cheating, it makes no difference to me." His eyes moved up slowly and locked with mine. "But if you want my help, you're going to have to trust me and tell me whatever it is I want to know." He paused and for just one brief moment, his eyes glanced at my mouth. Immediately, they were back, focused on my eyes, but it didn't go unnoticed. "I could walk out of here and take any number of cases. I could find any number of people who won't question me or act suspiciously when I ask perfectly reasonable questions. So," he stated finally, "I'll only ask one more time before I get up and leave you to find someone else willing to put up with your doubts. What makes you think he's cheating on you?"

I took in a deep breath, but never moved my eyes from his.

"I'll tell you whatever you want to know, but first, you have to understand that what I'm about to say, I've never told another living soul. It's a secret I thought, without a tiny sliver of doubt, I'd take to my grave. I have to believe this is confidential."

"I'm in the business of secrets, sweetheart."

I tried to ignore the arousal that pooled in my core at him calling me sweetheart, tried not to give any weight to the fact that my heart thundered in my chest, and tried to mumble my next statement with my voice unaffected.

"Marrying Derrek was the worst mistake I ever made. I was young. I was foolish, and I stupidly believed in our 'happily ever after'. I can pinpoint, to the second, when my idiocy imploded, and I will forever feel the ripples and after-effects of that one moment in time."

He lifted his glass again, this time taking a gulp of his scotch, draining it, then nodding to the waiter again, signaling he'd like another.

"Go on, Lena."

Chapter Five

"The night before our wedding, literally minutes before Derrek left our condo to spend the evening with his buddies, Derrek handed me a packet of papers and told me he needed me to sign them. I looked at them, glanced at them really, and saw he'd handed me a prenuptial agreement." I stopped to take a sip of my martini, hoping Preston didn't notice my hand was trembling slightly. I looked back to him and saw he was patiently waiting for me to finish my admission. So I took a deep breath and dove into the story.

"We'd never spoken about having a prenup, not once. So I was obviously caught a little off guard and had a few questions about why and how. Looking back on that evening, I think I acted well within reason – a bride is handed a prenup out of nowhere the night before her wedding, it's her prerogative to flip out a little. Derrek was telling me just to sign it and get it over with, that he had to go, had things to do, but I couldn't just *sign* a prenup. The discussion elevated to a full-on fight, with both of us screaming at each other, both of us using the same piece of logic to argue our very different opinions." I took in another deep breath and then pushed it out, trying not to let the emotions of that one evening so long ago seep into my reality now.

"I kept asking him, 'If you don't ever see us getting divorced, then why should I have to sign this?' And he kept asking me, 'If you don't ever see us getting divorced, then why *don't* you sign it?'" I shook my head at the memory, looking down at my hands resting on the tabletop. "It was a cyclical fight, one that we fought for over an hour, yelling at each other. The fight only ended when I picked up the pen and signed the papers, stupidly, without reading them thoroughly." A small laugh escaped my lips, surprising even me. "Thinking about it now, the fight was probably part of his plan. He needed to distract me somehow, get me riled up about something, push me so far that I'd do something so entirely stupid, and it worked. Here I am. Trying to fight against that stupid piece of paper I signed so long ago – a young bride hoping for a fairytale."

"What did the contract say about cheating?" Preston's voice was soft, which surprised me, causing me to look up into his eyes, and his face matched his voice. Softness.

"The prenup states, which I didn't find out until two years later when I finally grew a brain cell and looked at it, that if I divorced him for any reason, other than adultery, I would leave the marriage with exactly what I came into it with. Which, to be clear, was absolutely nothing."

Preston was quiet for a moment, his thumb running back and forth over the side of his glass. "So you think he's cheating, and you need me to get proof so you don't walk away empty handed?"

"I already have proof," I stated quickly. "What I need you to find is solid proof. Irrefutable proof." I leaned closer to him. "I refuse to walk away with nothing. I've spent the last seven years supporting him, helping him build his business, being the picture-perfect wife, and I'll be damned if he gets to keep everything."

"Careful," he said quietly. "You'll start to sound like the bitter, jilted wife."

"Maybe I am the bitter, jilted wife."

"What does the contract say about you?"

"What do you mean?"

"I mean, what are the stipulations regarding your extramarital affairs?"

"Same. If he walks away for any reason other than adultery, he forfeits everything to me. Except, if I cheat on him, I'm on the line for punitive damages. I'd be left with nothing except a bill for one hundred thousand dollars."

"And what if you can prove he's cheating?"

"Half. Of everything."

"So, he cheats you get half. You cheat you owe one hundred grand."

"That pretty much sums it up."

"So, have you?"

"Have I what?"

"Cheated?"

"That's none of your business, and has no bearing on what I'm hiring you to investigate."

"Yeah, but I'm interested as fuck."

Hearing him say 'fuck' sent shocks of electricity through my veins – another primal reaction to him I desperately wanted to ignore. But I wanted to hear him say that word over and over again, wanted to watch his lips caress that word. I crossed my legs under the table, trying to relieve some of the pressure that was starting to build there. He watched me squirm and I might have seen his eyes shift from curiosity to excitement.

"Well, you'll have to live in your curiosity, because my sex life is none of your concern."

"Fine, have it your way, sweetheart," he said as he took another sip of his scotch. "You say you've already got proof of his infidelity. So why, exactly, am I here?"

"All I've got is my word, and if I've got nothing and he's got everything, he'll be able to hire lawyers to tear me and my word apart."

"And what's your word?"

"Pardon?"

"You say you've got your word? What does your word say? What's your proof?"

"I saw him."

"Saw him?"

"Yes. Derrek hasn't been coming home lately, been staying out late or not coming back to the house at all. So a few nights ago, my girlfriend and I followed him when he got off work. We tailed him to a house about an hour out of the city where he was met by a woman with two small children. The children looked to be very familiar with him and he looked very familiar with the woman as he kissed her right on her porch."

"You're right," he stated flatly.

"Right about what?"

"That story would never get you anywhere."

"It's not a story, it's the truth, but you're not telling me anything I didn't already know. I need more proof."

"You think the children are his?"

I thought about the little girl running and jumping into his arms and him lifting her over his head, his beautiful smile pulling across his face at her laughter. A lump caught in my throat and I nodded. "Yeah, I think they're his."

"So, he isn't just cheating on you, he's got a whole other fucking life."

My core clenched again at the word 'fucking' passing over his lips. My body's reaction to him was ridiculous, and even though I tried my hardest to fight it, I felt my cheeks flushing, my skin heating. My body should have been reacting to his proclamation, the fact my husband had another life, another woman at his side. Instead, my thighs were clenching together trying to calm the pulsing between them.

"That's what I'm hiring you to find out," I whispered. He was quiet for a moment as he stared at me over the table. His face was unreadable. I had absolutely no idea as to what he was thinking. But his stare was heavy and with every second his eyes burned into me, I felt my pulse race faster.

"The retainer's two thousand," he finally said, coldly. I swallowed then blinked.

"That's fine." I reached into my purse and pulled out my checkbook.

"You can't write a check. Your husband would figure you out in a heartbeat. Can you get a hold of cash?"

I hadn't even thought about that. I racked my brain for ways to come up with two thousand dollars without Derrek getting suspicious. I'd have to ask Samantha.

"I can have cash for you in the next couple of days. Is that all right?"

"That's fine." Suddenly, he picked up my phone and started touching the screen.

"What are you doing?"

"I called you from my work number. Odds are you won't be able to reach me there, so don't even bother. I'll give you my private cell number and you call me when you've got the money. Until then, I'll start working on this." He handed my phone back to me. "But if you find something out, anything you think might be useful, don't hesitate to call me."

"Okay," I said softly. "So, that's it? You just go on your merry way and I sit around while you prove my husband is a cheating bastard?"

"Was there something else you wanted from me?" His face was stoic as he said those words and his eyes bore into me, asking a question heavy with so much meaning. I tried to swallow but found my mouth and throat dry, goose bumps rising on my arms.

"No," I whispered, some part of me knowing I was telling possibly the biggest lie of all. A quiet moment passed where our eyes held each other's. Then, so quickly, it was over. He stood and pulled his wallet out of his back pocket, tossing a hundred dollar bill on the table, then folded his wallet and put it away again.

"I'll be in touch." Those were his last words before he turned and walked right out the door. I let out a loud breath and collapsed against the back of my chair, not realizing I'd been upright and tense. I brought a shaky hand to my forehead and brushed my hair back, smoothing away nothing because I knew my hair was perfect. My hands were just looking for something to do besides the very thing they wanted to do, which was slide down my thighs and give attention to the ache that was still pulsing in my core.

I hoped, if only for my sanity, that Preston Reid was as good at his job as he was good looking. The less time I spent around him, the better. He was bad news, but I was beginning to understand that my body liked bad.

Chapter Six

The next day, after my body had calmed down, I called Sam and asked her over for lunch. Once she arrived, she wasted no time expressing her anger toward me.

"I told you to call, Lena."

"And I did. You're here, aren't you?" I didn't bother looking at her as I spoke; I was busy building us sandwiches. I knew she'd be over her tiff in a few minutes anyway. She just needed a few to harp on me and all would be well again.

"Two days later! I texted you a million times. I even came by earlier today but you didn't answer the door."

"I was out."

"Yeah, I figured," she said snidely.

I turned and handed her a plate with a BLT and some macaroni salad. "Let's go sit on the deck." I motioned with my head toward the sliding door that would lead us outside to a wrought iron table and chairs. Once seated, Sam dove right back in.

"So, what's happened since you discovered your husband is the biggest asshole on the planet?" She finished her sentence and took a big bite of her sandwich, her eyes locked on mine.

I laughed because I loved how much she hated Derrek, and because of how ready she was to simply kick his ass.

"I've got a plan in place. Actually, that's one of the things I need to talk to you about." I paused and tried to work up the nerve to ask my best friend for a loan. A loan she would know I didn't need, so it had to come with an explanation. "Yesterday, I hired a private investigator to look into Derrek and his other life."

"Why do you need a private investigator? We *saw* him, Lena. We already know he's cheating."

"I know, Sam, trust me. I know. But I want more. I need to know how long it's been going on, how deep it goes. I know it might seem masochistic, but I just need to know." I shook my head a little and looked down at my hands in my lap. I couldn't tell her about the prenup. I was so ashamed that it even existed and I didn't need her pity. I looked up at her. She already had a sad look on her face, and I knew it was sadness for me, and that was more than enough pity. "There's one other thing, though." I took in another deep breath. "I went to pay him with a check and he refused, saying that if I used a check, Derrek would catch on. For the same reason, I can't really withdraw the money from our bank account, so I was hoping–"

"How much do you need?"

"Two thousand," I said, as I winced.

"Done. I'll go to the bank today."

I sagged in my chair with relief. "Oh, my gosh, Sam, thank you so much. I promise I will get you the money. It just might take a week or two."

"Don't worry about it. Honestly, I'm glad to help." She paused for a moment, then tilted her head to the side and narrowed her eyes. "I can't believe you hired a private investigator. How did you even find one?"

"Google," I said with a laugh. "It wasn't difficult at all."

"So, you just call them up and tell them what you need?"

"Well, basically, except we met in person to discuss specifics."

"Oh." Then her face scrunched up and she sat back further in her chair. "I can't believe you met a P.I. without me." She frowned and I laughed.

"I didn't think it was a group activity."

"It totally was. It's like something out of an action movie. Your life just got so exciting and I want to be there to watch everything unfold." I raised an eyebrow at her. "You know what I mean! I'm not glad your husband is a cheating bastard, but I am happy to watch him go down in flames."

I could understand her point of view. Even I was looking forward to watching Derrek's other world crumble. "Well, the next time I have reason to call a private investigator, I'll be sure I conference you in."

"So, what's he going to do? How is he going to earn his two grand?"

I bit my bottom lip, then opened my mouth to reply, but promptly shut it again when I realized I didn't have an answer. "You know what? I'm not quite sure. I didn't really ask him what his plans were."

"See, just one of the reasons you should have brought me with you. I would have asked all the pertinent questions."

"Okay," I said with a small laugh. "I'm beginning to see the error of my ways." We continued eating our lunch with our usual light conversation, only sometimes venturing to talk about Derrek and what we'd seen, or Preston and what we thought he might be up to. Our imaginations were more than likely a lot more interesting than the actual happenings. But when Sam focused on something, she really focused. She seemed to be convinced that Preston was more like a James Bond than the image of a normal cop deciding to branch out on his own, which was what I believed to be more likely. Although, Preston was devastatingly handsome, so I gave Sam that tick in the Bond column.

We had just started clearing the table when the doorbell sounded throughout the house. I put down the dishes in my hand and walked toward the front door. When I opened it, I was immediately confused and stammered my greeting.

"Preston…Mr. Reid…What are you…How did you…"

"Good afternoon, Lena." His voice was flat and all business.

"How do you know where I live?"

At that, he smiled. It was a sardonic smile, as if he were laughing at me, but it was still breathtaking. "I'm a private investigator, sweetheart. It's my job to acquire information."

Why in the world did he keep calling me that? It was not only unprofessional, but also flustered me and left me mumbling like an idiot.

"What…why…?"

"I was hoping I could take a peek in your husband's office. See if there's anything in there that might aid my investigation."

"Right. Of course. Come in, please." I stepped back, opening the door to let him in. He walked past me and I tried so very hard not to notice that he smelled divine. Clean, with a hint of spice, from an aftershave perhaps. It wasn't overpowering, but just strong enough to penetrate my thoughts and make me want to smell that scent forever.

He stopped just a few steps in, waiting for me to lead him back to Derrek's office, and just then, Sam walked into the foyer.

"Oh," she said with surprise. Her eyes roamed all over Preston and I watched as she came to the same conclusion any straight woman with a pulse would – he was absolutely beautiful.

He was still sporting his black leather jacket, but he was dressed a little more casually underneath it than he'd been the day before. He wore a dark blue Henley t-shirt, coupled with the same faded jeans, but instead of his leather shoes, he had on black Converse.

"Who are you?" Sam asked, a little breathless, her eyes still taking in all of him.

"Sam, this is Mr. Reid, the private investigator I hired." Her eyes slowly made their way to mine, one eyebrow raised, a conspiratorial smile flashing across her mouth.

"Well, now I see why you didn't want me to come with you."

I glared at her, but tried my best to ignore her comment. "You can follow me, Mr. Re–"

"Preston, please. Call me Preston."

"All right. This way, Preston. Derrek's office is back this way." I headed down the hall and made my way back to the office, trying not to think about the fact that Preston was behind me, in my house, and that we were essentially alone together. And I definitely tried not to think about the way he smelled.

I entered the office and stood in front of the desk as I watched him do his P.I. thing. He looked around the room and I had no idea what it was he thought he'd find, but he was intent. He walked to stand behind Derrek's desk and opened up the first drawer on the right side, and frowned. Then he bent a little lower, opened the drawer beneath it, and then frowned again.

"The drawers are empty," he said with confusion.

"Oh. Yes. I might have thrown some things away," I said, trying not to sound as embarrassed as I was.

"You *might* have thrown some things away?" His voice had a smile to it, but he was busy opening and closing empty drawers.

"The night we followed Derrek and saw him with his other family, I came home and needed to relieve some stress."

"So you threw away some papers?" His question came with a chuckle.

His words made my back straighten. He was laughing at me.

"First, I threw them all over the room, *then* I threw them in the garbage."

He was trying to keep the smirk from his face, I could tell. "So you came home, emptied his drawers in a fit of rage, scattering his documents all over the room, and then you cleaned up your mess?"

He was definitely laughing at me.

I narrowed my eyes at him.

"What are you getting at?" I sneered.

He came from behind the desk and walked toward me. For just a moment, his eyes were on mine, but then they moved to the wall behind me where Derrek had his diplomas displayed. He passed me, but left no room between us, his arm brushing my shoulder, but then I felt him turn sharply so he was just behind me, slightly pressed up against me. I stiffened when I felt his front graze my back. I lost the ability to breathe when I felt his breath against my ear as he spoke.

"I'm just saying," he practically growled. "There are better, more gratifying ways to release your aggression." I felt him move away, but the absence of him made no difference to the storm that was now brewing inside my traitorous body. I was stunned silent, my heart pulsing through my body, pumping blood to areas suddenly awakened by his breath on my skin. For the second time in just as many days, I found myself pressing my thighs together, trying to stave off the physical reaction I was having to Preston. My breath shuddered out of me, not quietly, and I winced, thinking he had heard and could tell I was affected by him. Although, it wouldn't take a rocket scientist to figure out I was aroused; my entire body seemed to be quivering.

I tried to be angry at him, tried to be appalled that he, the supposed professional in our arrangement, would be hitting on me, a married woman. But even though the notion was there, the intention to find his actions repulsive, I couldn't move past my acute arousal.

"I think," I managed to say, although I sounded completely unsure of my words and not at all as forceful as I imagined I would in my mind, "I think you need to leave."

"Why's that?" His voice was still behind me, but I turned to see him inspecting the certificates on the wall.

"What if Derrek returns? How will I explain a strange man in his office? In his home?"

He turned back around, but didn't look at me. He moved again, heading to the big chair behind the desk and sat down, powering on the computer. "You obviously have no faith in me and my ability to do my job. Why in the world did you even hire me?"

"Your company was just the first one I came to," I answered honestly. He nodded but didn't speak immediately. He pressed some buttons on the computer then spoke again.

"You hired me to investigate your husband and his extracurricular activities. He is currently in Bend. Whether he's there for business or pleasure, I'm not sure."

"Then shouldn't you be there trying to *investigate* that?"

His eyes snapped to me and his voice was smooth but dark. "Would you like to pay me six hundred dollars, each way, to follow your philandering husband on a ski weekend?" He paused and watched me. I tried not to give away that no, I did not want to pay him twelve hundred dollars to drive to Bend, but I wouldn't give him the satisfaction.

Instead, I turned and left the room, throwing over my shoulder, "Let me know if you need anything else." I continued back into the kitchen, where I found Sam leaning her hip against the counter, one hand to her mouth, unconsciously biting her nails.

"Holy shit, Lena," she said loudly when I walked in. "You did not tell me your private investigator is the most attractive man I've ever seen in person."

"Keep your voice down!" I whispered to her. The very last thing I needed was Preston Reid hearing us talk about how attractive he was. "And he is *not* the most attractive person you've ever seen," I countered.

She scoffed at me. "He abso-fucking-lutely is the hottest man I have ever encountered."

"You had your eyes on him for all of ten seconds," I said as I moved past her, trying to busy myself with cleaning the kitchen, needing a distraction.

"I only needed three," she replied. "What are you going to do?"

"What do you mean?"

"What are you going to do about the man in your husband's office who exudes sexual prowess?"

"Sam, you're being ridiculous. I've hired him to investigate my cheating husband, that's all."

"So you're not even going to try to see him naked?"

"What? No! I'm married."

"You're married to a man who has another woman on the side with whom he has two children." This was information I already had, but hearing someone else say the words so callously hurt.

"That doesn't mean I'm going to jump the first attractive man I come across."

"So you think he's attractive?" Sam asked, her voice more amused than it should have been.

"Excuse me, Lena?"

Both Sam and I twisted when we heard Preston's voice shoot through the room, and saw him standing in the entryway, the smirk on his face alluding to the fact he'd heard our conversation.

Shit.

"What can I help you with?" I asked.

"I need to look in your bedroom."

"My bedroom? What for?"

"You really don't understand how this whole investigative thing works, do you? I just need to look around, see if there's anything that piques my interest."

"You think he left clues to his affair in our bedroom?"

He shrugged in response.

I sneered at him again, but then moved to lead him to my bedroom.

"I'm going to head to the bank real quick to get you that money, Lena," I heard Sam call out as I walked down the hall.

"All right," I called back. I turned back to Preston. "She's going to loan me the retainer, so if you're still here when she gets back, you can have your money."

"She seems like a good friend."

"She is," I said, facing forward again.

"Does she know? About the prenup, I mean?" he asked gently.

"Preston, like I said yesterday, you're the only person I've ever told about that." I sighed and stopped outside my bedroom door, motioning with my hand. I didn't want to spend time in my and my husband's bedroom with another man. It didn't seem right – it felt cheap and wrong. But it also felt exciting and, for that, I decided not to go in. "I'll be in the kitchen if you need anything," I said quietly, and then left him to do his private investigating.

In the kitchen, I continued to clean what was left from our lunch and then, for the second day in a row, decided to indulge in a drink. Not feeling like putting in too much effort, I simply grabbed some orange juice from the refrigerator and poured some in a glass, then added a generous portion of vodka. I sat down on one of the barstools that lined the long side of the island and listened for sounds of Preston rummaging through my marriage.

I couldn't imagine what he thought he would find in our bedroom that I might not have seen, might not have caught on to. He wouldn't find any evidence of a loving relationship; that was for sure. There would be no sexy underwear in the hamper, no rumpled sheets on the bed. No, I imagined from his perspective he would see a very sterile room and pity my husband for having such a frigid wife.

I was halfway through my drink when I heard him come back into the kitchen.

"I think I'm about through here. Sorry for the intrusion."

I got the feeling he was referring to more than just interrupting lunch.

"It's no problem. Find what you were looking for?"

"Not sure yet," he said, seriously, his eyes locked on to mine. I simply couldn't handle his eyes on me, not when they were full of words that I felt he wanted to say but held back. No, it was time to say goodbye to Preston Reid.

"Sam isn't back yet, but I'll be sure to get you the money soon. I could drop it by the office later today if that's more convenient for you."

"No, don't take it to the office. I'll be in contact. I'm not worried about the money."

"All right," I said. "Let me walk you to the door." I stood and made my way past him, leading him back into the foyer. I reached for the door handle but stopped when I heard his voice again.

"Was staying with him this long, suffering through what seems like a loveless marriage, really worth the money you're fighting for now?"

I stared at him, trying not to let my face give away the array of emotions his question sent spinning around in my head.

"I didn't realize, until just recently, I was in a loveless marriage." I looked him straight in the eye, my face expressionless, steeled to look void of anything. Without removing my eyes from him, I turned the doorknob and opened the door. He obviously took my silence as the only farewell he would be getting and he walked through.

I tried not to notice that even though he had plenty of room, he passed so close to me that I felt his shoulder brush me again. I also tried to ignore what his scent did to me, as well as the jolt that zipped through me when my body touched his.

Chapter Seven

The next night, I laid in bed and listened for Derrek to return. Preston hadn't said whether Derrek had gone to Bend alone. I wasn't even sure he knew, but I had spent over a day imagining the happy couple enjoying a short weekend getaway. Perhaps he'd taken his youngest to her first skiing lesson, watching her wobble and fall in the soft snow, her nose turning pink from the cold.

I had always told Derrek I wanted children, and he'd always gone to great lengths to convince me that we had time. He wanted to focus on his job and he needed me to help him with that aspect of our life. I wasn't, by any means, past my prime, and still had a few good baby-making years left in me. But knowing he'd started a family with someone else, that he'd taken my ability to start a family hostage, left my heart pumping in an empty chest. I was angry, but more so, I was hurt.

I'd always imagined having a few babies. I'd daydreamed about holding the warm bundles in my arms, snuggling them, kissing them, but now I was left with nothing. Well, nothing besides a cheating husband who planned to keep me around for a reason only

God could understand. That wasn't true either – he kept me around so he didn't lose his precious money.

My eyes widened as a new thought occurred to me. Did the other woman know about me? I wanted to believe that she didn't, that she couldn't. I hoped she was just as blind to his transgressions as I had been. I didn't want to think one woman could do that to another. At this point, the sisterhood was the only thing in which I had any faith left.

I heard the door open and I stopped breathing, as the sound of my breaths was interfering with my ability to hear the faint sounds of him entering the house. I listened as he closed the door and then I heard some rustling, which I figured was him setting his things down. When I heard his footsteps head down the hall toward his office, I let out my breath quietly. My lungs were burning and my heart was pounding. I took in a few gulping breaths to try to let my lungs relax, and then, before I knew what I was doing and could stop myself, I pulled the covers back and walked down the stairs toward Derrek.

When I made it to the doorway, I stalled, still unwillingly captivated by how handsome he was. He was standing behind his desk, pulling the tie loose from around his neck. He was wearing gray suit pants with a shiny black belt, a white button up shirt that looked wrinkled, as if he'd been wearing it for a while, and the tie he was pulling from his neck was black as well.

"You're home," I said softly. I hadn't intended to speak to him. Hell, I hadn't intended to walk down here at all. But I was also acutely aware that I wasn't fully in control of my mind, body, or mouth at the moment.

"It would seem so," he said, without meeting my eyes.

"Where did you go?"

"Out of town on business." His words were cold, stale, and stone-like. I tried to read into them, tried to figure out whether he was lying and discern if he'd really been away for pleasure. His eyes still weren't meeting mine as he sat down in his chair and put his thumb and forefinger up to the bridge of his nose, pinching it.

"Did you get a lot done?" My voice was calm and smooth. Part of me was still hoping he'd been away on business.

"Lena…"

He didn't want to talk.

"Will you be coming to bed?" I had no idea why I asked that question. There were two reasons why that question was completely unnecessary. One: I already knew the answer was no. I already knew he wouldn't be coming to our bed. He would probably never be in that bed again, and I knew that. And two: I didn't want him in our bed. I was almost sure I didn't want him in our bed. What I wanted was to go to sleep and wake up, having the last five years of my life be a sick and twisted nightmare. I wanted to wake up to the husband who I loved, the husband who honored our vows, and didn't sneak away for weekend getaways with other women and his love children.

He didn't want to talk. So he didn't. He never answered my question, just clicked his computer on and continued to ignore me, pretending to be interested in whatever had appeared on his screen.

Watching him completely shut me out flipped some sort of switch inside my body. The very last piece of me that was holding out for some sort of understanding, some sort of resolution that included saving my marriage, faded away right into the darkness that filled every room of our house.

I turned and walked back up the stairs and climbed into my cold bed, falling into sleep as I contemplated how I was going to move forward. Unfortunately, all of those thoughts circled around Preston Reid.

The next day, I went to work as if it were any other day of the week. I had a comfortable position at a lucrative and expanding marketing firm in Portland. Derrek would have preferred me to sit on the board of a charity, or spend my time doing more social activities, making connections, networking with wives of powerful men, but I always stood firm on having my own career.

I was halfway through the day, mindlessly tending to all the catch-up from the weekend, when I heard my phone vibrating in the top drawer of my desk. I pulled the phone out and slid my finger across the screen, revealing I had a new text message. It was from Preston.

I need you tonight.

I read the words and tried to keep my pulse under control. Then I admonished myself for allowing my body to react so powerfully to his words. I gaped at my phone and felt my core pulsing with every beat of my heart, which was rapid and ferocious. I swallowed, but still didn't move, uncertain of what my next move even was. Before I was forced to make a decision, my phone vibrated again.

I can be at your house to pick you up around five.

What in the world was he talking about? I was still trying to recover from his first text, also trying to keep my mind from running away with those words and turning them into something completely inappropriate.

What, exactly, do you need me for?

I felt my breathing even out as I waited for a response. There was no hope to focus on anything else until he responded. After what seemed like a millennium, his answer came.

Lena, there are many things I need you for. The list is long, involved, and dirty. But tonight, I need you for professional reasons. However, if you wish to rearrange the parameters of our relationship, I am open to that discussion.

Holy shit. He was flirting with me. Well, if one could call that flirting. He was flat out propositioning me. My hand, of its own accord, came to the base of my neck, trailing across my collarbone. I thought about my options for a moment, and even though I tried, desperately, to keep my mind on the task at hand – finding inarguable proof that Derrek was cheating – my mind wandered to Preston's dark eyes and luscious lips. My fingertips trailed down my sternum and then back up my neck, the tickling sensation making goose bumps appear wherever my skin was bare. Then my phone buzzed again and I jerked my eyes to the screen.

Sweetheart, are you with me?

Oh, God.

I'm here.

I replied without meaning to.

Will you be ready at five?

I swallowed hard and my fingers moved over the screen.

I'll be ready.

At five sharp, I watched as a very sleek, very sexy, black Lotus pulled into my driveway. I continued to watch as the driver's door opened and Preston unfolded himself from it. He was still wearing that sexy jacket and I wondered if he ever went anywhere without it, or even took it off. He had a dark blue t-shirt stretched over his chest, just tight enough to hint at what was beneath it, and a pair of black jeans. He walked toward my front door and I forced myself to stop peering at him through the living room blinds.

I stood and brushed my hands down my front, making sure I looked presentable. When I heard the doorbell ring, I continued to the door, opening it right after I took a calming breath. In through the nose, out through the mouth.

When the door was open, we both just stood there, neither one of us able to hide the fact that our eyes roamed the other.

"You're not dressed appropriately." He spoke first, his eyes still running up and down my body.

I looked down at my outfit. "What do you mean?" I was wearing jeans and a soft, white, short-sleeved sweater.

"I mean," he said, stepping into my house, forcing me to step back and allow him entrance, "you can't wear that. Go change into something dark, like black. We can't have you standing out."

"Where are we going?"

"We're going to follow Derrek home from work. I'm hoping he'll head to his *other* home."

Well, that stung.

I nodded out the door to his black car with very dark tinted windows. "I don't think anyone will be able to see me through your windows."

The corners of his mouth turned up slightly, not a full smile, but a hint of one. He turned and walked further into the house, forcing me to follow.

"Who says we'll stay in the car?"

I guess he had me there. "I'll be right back," I mumbled, grudgingly. When I returned, I looked much the same as I did when Sam and I did our stakeout. I was in black jeans, but instead of the turtleneck, I wore a black, V-neck cotton tee. The jersey knit hugged my chest and I purposefully chose it over the frumpy turtleneck. If I had to look at Preston in his leather jacket and blue, clingy shirt, he would have to endure my tee that gave a slight view of my cleavage. He looked at me when I reentered the room, but quickly motioned toward the front door.

"Let's get a move on. We don't have much time."

The ride to Derrek's work was silent, and I was okay with that. I spent my time trying to figure out what all the buttons did inside Preston's Lotus. It looked how I imagined the inside of a space shuttle might: flashing lights, switches, buttons everywhere, and even my ass was warm. He parked across the street from the main door, just like Sam had, and we sat and watched, waiting for him to come out. I was in the middle of wishing we had snacks when Derrek walked out. My breath caught in my throat as we silently watched him walk to his car, and I managed to exhale when he pulled out into traffic. Preston pulled out after him, but we didn't talk as he tailed him.

Preston was noticeably better at following a car than Sam and I had been. He didn't need me to tell him where to go, or which direction Derrek's car was heading, as he seemed to manage both the tailing and driving aspects fairly well on his own. So well, in fact, I began to wonder why he'd even brought me along.

"Why am I here?"

"What do you mean? You want to get your proof, right?"

"Yeah, but I'm obviously not needed. I haven't said one word and you haven't asked me one question. I'm not aiding your investigation one bit. So why did you bring me?"

"Where did you meet him?" he asked, keeping his eyes on the road and presumably Derrek's car.

"What?"

"Your husband. Where did you meet him?"

"How is that going to help your investigation?"

He shrugged. "It won't. You just seem a little uptight so I thought I'd give you what you want – a little interaction."

I eyed him, trying to decide whether I was going to answer his question. I finally rolled my eyes and gave him the answer. "I met him at a frat party my sophomore year of college."

"Hmm," was his response.

"Hmm?"

"I could totally see Derrek as a frat guy, but you, well, you don't strike me as the kind of girl who hangs out with them." As he said this, his head swiveled toward me and his eyes were gleaming, a slight smile pulling up the corners of his mouth.

"I wasn't, really," I said, turning away from him again. "Sam dragged me there and I was holding up a wall, drinking alone, when Derrek approached me."

"And then he swept you off your feet?"

It was my turn to shrug. "I suppose. I mean, it's not like we were engaged the next day or anything, but I never dated anyone else after I met him that night."

"How old were you?"

"Nineteen."

"That's not a lot of time to cram in a lot of dating experience."

"I hadn't had any." The words came tumbling from my mouth and I wanted to reach out and grab each and every one before he'd had a chance to hear them. I cringed inwardly. Preston cleared his throat and shifted in his seat, obviously uncomfortable with my careless and inappropriate confession, and then suddenly, I realized I wasn't familiar with my surroundings any longer. "I don't think he's heading to the same house as he did the other night."

"What makes you say that?" he asked, and I couldn't help but think he was glad for the sudden change in subject.

"This isn't the same route. Last time, we left his building and made our way straight to the freeway. He's definitely heading somewhere different."

"Do you remember which freeway he took?"

"Yes. He took I-84, headed East."

Before I knew what was happening, Preston slid his souped-up Lotus around the next corner, hanging a right so sharp I was forced to lean to my left, and centrifugal force had me leaning right into Preston's shoulder. My hands reached out to the sides, trying to find purchase on any surface that would keep me upright.

"What the hell, Preston?" I shouted as the car straightened out. My heartbeat was thundering and I looked to him, searching for an explanation.

"If I get us to the freeway, can you get me to the house again?"

"You mean his other house with his other wife and children?"

"Yeah. Can you get me there?"

I blinked at him, my eyes narrowing, eyebrows scrunching together. Somehow, in the last thirty seconds, he'd gone from somewhat aloof, asking me pointless questions, to this high-strung man making demands and full of tension.

"Yea…yes, I think I can get you there," I stammered.

Again, we were thrust into silence as he navigated his way to the interstate. When we'd been driving for nearly thirty minutes, I recognized our exit and then proceeded to direct him back to the house.

We pulled up and drove by slowly. The house was dark and seemed empty. It was only early evening and it seemed unlikely that someone was inside, considering how dark it was. Preston kept driving, but at the next intersection, he made a U-turn and then pulled over a few houses down the road. We sat in silence and I stole glances at Preston, waiting for his next move.

"What are we doing here?" I whispered. No one could hear me but him, but it felt like a situation that warranted whispering.

"Investigating," he said slowly, his eyes still on the house.

"But no one's here," I whispered in response.

"That's where the private comes into play." This he said with a small smile, and damn it if I couldn't help a smile coming across my face as well. I let the smile settle. It caused a little bit of tension to roll away, and I relaxed into the lush seats of his fancy car. For a few more minutes we sat in the quiet car. Preston's eyes were locked on the house and then finally he reached down an unbuckled his seatbelt.

"What are you doing?"

"*We're* going into the house."

"Oh, no, we're not," I stated loudly, a little surprised he would even consider it.

"The proof you're so desperate for might be inside that house, Lena. Do you think he's just going to hand it to you? You think he's just going to give up and hand you half of a fortune he feels one-hundred-percent entitled to? You hired me to find you proof, and this is how we're going to get it. Now, get out of the car and follow me."

My mouth gaped open for a moment, then I snapped it shut. He was right. We wouldn't get the proof I needed sitting in his car. I unclicked my seatbelt and opened the door, shutting it softly behind me, not wanting to draw attention to us. I met Preston at the front of his car and gasped when his hand folded around mine and laced our fingers together. He tugged gently on my hand, pulling me into his side, and he pushed our clasped hands behind me, pressing them into my lower back.

The front of me was fully pressed against his side and his warm fingers were wrapped around mine. I was sure he could hear my heartbeat pounding through my body, and I instinctively pressed my free hand into his chest, trying and failing to push him away. He was too close. He felt too good. I was tugged a little closer and felt his lips on the shell of my ear.

"Don't pull away, sweetheart." His breath floated over my skin and I bit my lip to hold in a moan, still fighting my body for control, fighting the reaction I was having. "If anyone is watching us, we simply look like a couple taking an evening stroll." His mouth lingered and I relaxed. I told myself I was playing along, not wanting to draw attention. Really, I took the opportunity to feel him. My hand on his chest moved slightly, running along the valley between his pectoral muscles. His body was hard and warm, my fingers grazing along his front. His hand gently squeezed mine behind my back, silently reassuring me. My hand moved up over his shoulder, slowly cresting and ending up behind his neck, my fingers running over the softness of the close-shaved hair at the nape. He exhaled and I felt his forehead press into my temple.

"We're going to go in the house and you're going to keep watch, yeah?"

I nodded, but left my hand on his neck. I felt Preston's head tilt slightly, and then his lips were pressed against the sensitive skin just below my ear. My lungs quit working and all the synapses in my body fired at the same time, and I felt my stomach flip. His mouth was on me and it was glorious.

Then he was gone.

He kept a hold on my hand, pulling me toward the house I'd seen Derrek go into just days before. As we walked up the drive, Preston pulled something from his back pocket and when we reached the front door, he let go of my hand and crouched down. I did my duty and looked around, watching for anyone who might see us, and I heard the sound of the doorknob jiggling and metal scraping against metal. When I heard the door open, I turned and saw Preston slowly making his way inside.

My heart thundered so fiercely in my body, I wasn't sure I was going to survive. Never in my life had I done anything illegal, so breaking into someone's house was not something I was used to. When I stalled on the front porch, Preston came back for me, wrapping his hand around mine once again, and tugging me into the house, shutting the door behind me.

"Lena, breathe. Everything is going to be fine. No one is here."

I took his advice and dragged in a breath, doing my best not to pass out in the entryway. I nodded at him, but couldn't see his expression in the darkened house. He gave my hand a squeeze, but then let it go and moved away from me.

"Where are you going?" I whispered, this time the whisper totally justified.

"I'm going to investigate." I didn't have to see his face to know he was smiling. "You stay here and keep watch. If you see or hear anything suspicious, let me know."

"Okay."

He disappeared, the darkness swallowing him, but I could still hear him throughout the house. I stood at the door, peering out the windows next to it, watching for anything that might cause alarm. Minutes passed and my heart slowed and my body started to relax. A car came down the road and my breath caught, but when it slowly drove past, I relaxed again.

After a while of nothing exciting, I saw a person walking on the sidewalk across the street. They came from the right and when they were directly across from the house, they stopped and turned toward it and seemed to just stare. They were too far away for me to see clearly, but I knew the person was facing the house and not moving. When they didn't continue on their way, I panicked and went to find Preston.

"Preston," I whisper-shouted into the blackness. Not being familiar with my husband's other home, I was fumbling in the darkness, trying not to run into furniture or walls. "Preston!" I whisper-shouted again. I was walking down a hallway, peering into dim doorways, trying quietly to whisper his name.

I came to another door and noticed a figure moving inside the room.

"Preston?" I whispered.

"Yeah?" he said. I turned into the room and saw a beautiful four-poster king-sized bed. I halted just a few steps in, realizing I was in a bedroom. Most likely, *their* bedroom. A wave of nausea came over me, but was pulled away from it when a warm hand wrapped around my upper arm. "What is it?"

I blinked, trying to acclimate, trying to see him. "There's a person across the street watching the house."

He didn't respond right away, but his hand never left my arm.

"What did they look like?"

"I couldn't see them very well, what with the darkness and all," I said, with more snark than I probably needed. His hand ran down my arm to grasp mine and he led me to the side of the window. He pulled me next to him so our backs were both pressed against the wall and then he leaned over and peeked through the edge of the curtains. After a few seconds, he moved back next to me.

"There's no one out there now."

"Okay," I said, whispering still, suddenly very aware I was in a dark bedroom with Preston Reid. My pulse fluttered and I tried to remind myself I was in the bedroom my husband shared with his mistress. I tugged my hand from his grasp and started walking toward the hallway to resume my post at the front door.

Two things happened in the next few seconds. The first thing was I heard the front door opening down the hall. The unmistakable sound of the key in the deadbolt caused all my blood to freeze in my veins, along with the air in my lungs. The second thing that happened was me being swiftly lifted fully off my feet, with a strong arm wrapped around my waist, and hauled into a walk-in closet. My mouth opened, ready to scream, but then I remembered we were on a stealthy B&E, and clamped my mouth closed before any sound came out.

I was whisked into the closet and taken all the way to the back. Preston pushed aside shirts and sweaters, bringing us both behind the clothes, then fixed the hangers, trying to hide us. I found myself in the corner, my back pressed up against a wall, and Preston pressed up against my front. He was warm and tall, and magnificently hard. I felt all his muscles pressing against every single inch of my body, and my hands came to rest naturally on his chest, my eyes searching for his in the dark.

"Preston—" I started to object to his body pressing so deliciously into mine, but I felt his finger press into my lips, effectively shushing me. Something about his finger on my mouth sent my body into overdrive, and I squirmed against him, my traitorous body searching for more contact.

"No talking, sweetheart," he said, so quietly I wasn't even sure I'd heard it. But I felt his breath and the way his chest moved when he said 'sweetheart.' If I wasn't completely paralyzed already, I then heard Derrek's voice ringing through the house.

"Jessica, it's not a big deal. Just grab your purse and let's go."

Then I heard *her* voice.

"I'm sorry. I thought I had everything, but Elise threw the biggest fit when I was trying to leave the house and I must have just forgotten."

"It's really fine. I'm not mad. But if we don't leave soon, we'll actually be late instead of fashionably late."

Their voices were getting closer and closer until I realized they were in the bedroom and the only thing separating us was a row of neatly hung blouses and a closet door. At the realization of their nearness, Preston pressed into me further and my eyes fluttered closed when I felt his lips just barely touch mine. He didn't kiss me. He wasn't kissing me. Our lips only just barely grazed against one another, allowing our breaths to intermingle. When I realized he wasn't *going* to kiss me, I opened my eyes. His hands were over my head, pressed up against the wall I was leaning into. My hands were still on his chest, and one of his thighs had parted my knees and was pressed against me.

"Here it is, honey," I heard the woman, *Jessica*, say brightly.

"Great," Derrek replied. "I'm just going to change my tie. Sadie had some sort of muck on her hands when she grabbed it earlier."

My eyes grew wide when I realized Derrek was heading into the closet. When the door opened, a dim light spread across the large closet, coming from the bedroom. I gasped silently and then, even though I would have bet it not possible, Preston moved even closer to me. His hands slid further up the wall and he dipped his face down to rest in the crook of my neck, his front pressing against me even harder, and my hands slid around his back and up to grip his shoulders.

The sound of the closet door closing again came very quickly, as if Derrek had grabbed a tie and left almost immediately. Preston made no move to back away as we listened to the voices drift away down the hall and then, finally, we heard the front door open and close again. Only after we heard the deadbolt lock again did Preston move. But he didn't move away fully, just far enough so that we were back to the kissing-but-not-kissing stance.

"Lena," he whispered against my lips. I melted instantly. Simply liquefied. His hands came away from the wall, but only came to cup the sides of my face, but he was still not kissing me. I let him hold me like that for a few moments, let the feeling of his hands on my skin wash over me. I hadn't been touched by a man in months, and being touched by Preston was proving to be the most heavenly experience of my life, even if it was just his hands on my cheeks. I reveled in it, soaked it in.

Then, reluctantly, I let reality back in and pressed my hands against his chest again, urging him away from me.

"Preston, we can't do this," I said, no longer worried about the level of my voice, but still speaking quietly. He made no move to let me go, didn't move back even a centimeter. "Please, let me go," I begged quietly. I heard him inhale deeply, then he stepped away and all of a sudden, I was free of him, and I tried not to notice how cold I instantly was. I didn't say anything, just pressed past him and made my way back to the front door to keep watch. I figured Derrek and Jessica probably wouldn't be returning, but I needed an excuse to get away from him.

A few minutes later, he came out of the darkness and appeared by the door.

"Anyone else come by?" he asked coolly, as if he wasn't just pressed up against me in a dark closet.

"No."

"Let's go, then." He reached out, unlocked the door and walked out into the night.

I followed him out of necessity. "Aren't you going to relock the door?"

"Nope."

"But they'll know someone was here."

He shrugged. "Or they'll just think they forgot to lock it. Either way, I don't care."

"Hey," I nearly shouted. "You might not care what they think, or if they know someone was here, but I do, and last I checked, I wasn't paying you to cause problems."

"Last I checked, you haven't paid me *anything*."

I narrowed my eyes at him. "You know what I mean. If you cause suspicion, Derrek could catch on to everything." Preston, with his hands planted on his hips, looked down at the ground, and even from fifteen feet away, I could tell he was angry. I wasn't the resident lock picker; there was no way I could make it look like no one had been there. I needed him to snap out of it. "Please, Preston. Don't jeopardize me this way."

He sighed but walked toward the door again. I turned, watching him crouch and fiddle with the lock. I heard it click into place and he stood, walking back to his car without a glance at me. When he reached his car, he coldly said as he slid into the driver's seat, "Get in." It wasn't a request; it was a demand.

The part of me that had liquefied before heated again at his words, and I tried to keep my breathing even. He was obviously being a jerk, but again, my body didn't care.

I spent the car ride back to Portland trying to dissect my attraction to him. I wasn't even sure attraction was the right word. I wasn't attracted to him. I was pulled to him. Drawn to him. It didn't make any sense, not to me, anyway. He was almost the exact polar opposite of everything I'd ever told myself I wanted. Well, as far as I knew. I realized I didn't know much about him. All I really knew was he wore that black leather jacket like a second skin, he never looked bad in a pair of jeans, and his brown eyes were mesmerizing. Oh, and my body craved the proximity of his.

We said absolutely no words all the way back into the city, and when he pulled into my driveway, I opened the door and climbed out without breaking the silence. I drew in a sharp breath when I heard his door open and his footsteps coming in my direction. I did not, however, give him the satisfaction of turning around. I continued up the path to the door, only stopping to input the code in the keypad on the door.

"Lena." Just my name falling from his lips turned my stomach inside out. I shook it off, literally shaking my head from side to side, trying to give him a clear indication that I didn't want to hear what he had to say. Not surprisingly, he didn't listen. Instead, his hand wrapped around my elbow and he turned me, and then pulled me into his front, our faces only inches from one another again. One of his hands found its way to my cheek again and I resisted the urge to lean into it, to let myself *feel* something from a man again.

Everything I was trying to accomplish, Preston was single handedly and slowly going to ruin. I had only one goal at that moment and that was to prove my husband was a cheating, lying bastard, get what was owed to me, and move on with my life.

Preston Reid was threatening to me in more ways than one.

"We need to talk," he tried again.

"No," I said immediately. "You need to go home and finish this job on your own. Get me my proof and then we can just go our separate ways." I remembered that his money was on my kitchen table. "I'll go inside and get your money. Give me one moment."

"I don't want your money."

I halted at his words and turned to him, trying to be brave and act like I wasn't affected by him.

"I hired you to do a job, so you'll take the money. Unless you think I should hire someone else?" My eyes found his and even in the dim light from the streetlamps, I could still see the dark brown irises looking back at me. I thought, for just an instant, I saw panic flash through them, but just as quickly as the emotion flitted across them, it was gone.

"No. You don't need to hire anyone else. I'll get you your proof."

"Okay," I whispered. I opened the door and walked in, heading into the kitchen to find the envelope Sam had brought me with the two thousand dollars cash inside. I grabbed it from the counter and turned to walk back outside, only to find Preston inside my house, leaning against the doorframe of the kitchen. "Here," I said softly as I held the envelope out toward him.

He took the few steps toward me and when his eyes met mine, I was a little surprised to see sadness there. He took the money and tucked it into his back pocket. His chin tipped up in a nod that said 'Thanks.' I found manners winning out and I couldn't stop myself before I offered, "Would you like something to drink? Scotch, perhaps?"

"Neat," was his short response, and it rolled through me like a wave, his dark voice deep and gravelly.

I nodded and said, "I'll be right back." When I made it to the liquor cabinet in the formal living room, I leaned against the bar, gripping the edge tightly, trying to rein in the heat coursing through my body. This was ridiculous. The very last thing I needed right then was some wild, gravitational pull to a man who wasn't my husband. I didn't even want my husband. But what I really didn't need was some seriously sexy man tempting me into wagering my future life away. But I'd offered him scotch, so I'd get him scotch. Then I'd make him leave.

I set the tumbler down in front of him, noticing he'd made himself comfortable at the head of my dining room table. I sat in the chair to his right and sipped from my tumbler.

"You spend a lot of time in this big house all by yourself?" His question caught me off guard, but also offended me a little. I didn't like him insinuating that I was often alone. I could have many friends I spent time with, or a ton of hobbies that kept me out. Zumba. Pottery. Cooking class. Then I remembered I was the jilted wife who hired him to tail her husband and his mistress. I wasn't the poster child for happy, satisfied women.

"I have things I do. I jog sometimes. I see Sam often. I'm not a shut-in."

He looked at me over the rim of his glass as he sipped his scotch. After a beat, he pulled the glass from his mouth and placed it slowly on the tabletop. "That's not what I meant," he said, his voice low again.

"Well, then please, elaborate."

"I meant does your husband leave you here alone often?"

His question threw me again, and I didn't know how to answer it. I suspected if I told him the truth, it might elicit a reaction from him I didn't want to deal with. Then again, I suspected if I lied to him, he'd know. In fact, the more I thought about it, the more I thought he already knew the answer to his question.

"Sometimes," was the answer I settled on.

"Sometimes?"

I shrugged, offering him nothing else.

"I don't like the idea of you being here alone."

His words cut right through the pretense I had been trying to build for the last hour and a half. Sliced right through the wall I'd put up. It had been years since a man had shown any kind of concern for me. I'd been on my own for so long, I couldn't have anticipated what it would feel like when a man, whom I apparently desired, showed concern for me. For whatever reason, Preston cared.

Before, in the closet, I could have written the whole ordeal off as physical – no, sexual – chemistry, but when he said things like that, basically telling me he cared about my well-being, there was no going back.

"I have an alarm," was my brilliant response.

"A man shouldn't leave his wife in a bed, alone, by herself, for any reason." He paused, perhaps waiting for me to interject, but I had no argument. I agreed with him. "Why do you put up with it?"

"I don't anymore."

"Hmm." His voice rumbled, even though he didn't really speak any words. "If you were mine, you'd never get a chance to even feel the sheets getting cold."

As if he'd reached inside, grabbed my breath, and dragged it from my body, I gasped.

"There wouldn't be a thing in this world that could keep me from my bed, were you in it."

He'd slayed me twice. A combo hit. TKO.

"Preston," I whispered, simply unable to piece any more words together than that. He didn't say another word, just slammed the rest of his scotch, got up, and walked out my door. I gaped after him, not sure what I was supposed to do. How does one recover from words like that?

Eventually I stood up, bringing both our empty glasses to the kitchen, placing the tumblers in the dishwasher. I walked to the foyer and punched in the passcode on the security panel, activating the alarm. I went upstairs and decided to take a long and very hot shower.

I spent most of my time in the shower replaying the entire evening, wondering how I'd gotten myself into such a strange situation. It might have been the longest shower I'd ever taken, and it took all the self-control I had not to slide my hand between my legs and replay the words he'd said to me over and over in my mind. I wasn't stupid enough to deny the fact my body wanted him – badly. But when everything else was said and done, I was still a married woman, and I wasn't sure I was ready to be a married woman who crossed those lines. And touching myself while thinking about another man wasn't something I thought was right to do, even though I really wanted to.

When I finally made it to bed, I pulled the covers back, bracing myself for cold sheets, then went to the window to close the curtains. Right before they closed all the way, I noticed the black Lotus sitting on the street just a few houses down.

Chapter Eight

When I woke up the next morning, Preston's car was gone. I tried not to think about him sitting in the Lotus all night keeping watch over my house because he cared about me. Nothing good could come from the warmth I felt in my chest when I thought about it, so I tried not to. It wasn't easy, especially because he came back every night for the rest of the week and kept watch over me.

Derrek hardly came home at all, and when he did, it was only for a few moments. He'd grab something and leave again, or pick up some mail he'd been expecting. Once or twice, he said something to me, but mostly, he wasn't even looking for me, only speaking to me if he happened to encounter me.

It took everything in me to not question him about Jessica, or let him know I knew what a scumbag he was, but I knew I had to bide my time. Eventually, I hoped I'd be able to tell him everything I wanted to. Right before I walked out the door forever.

On Thursday, after Derrek had come home and so brazenly packed an overnight bag, not even trying to convince me he was going away for business, I lost a little of my self-control and decided to call Preston for an update on the investigation. Surely, he'd have found something by then. I dialed his number and after a few rings, he answered with his deep voice, sending involuntary shivers up my spine.

"Reid," he said in greeting, his voice clipped but still sexy.

"It's me, Lena."

There was a pause, but then he spoke. "Is everything all right?"

"Yes, of course. I was just wondering if you've made any progress on the case." I heard a faint clicking in the background. "Are you in your car? Should I call you back?"

"No, it's fine. Bluetooth."

"Oh. Well? Any news?"

"Listen, Lena, I've been working on it, but another case has been taking up a lot of my time. It'll be a few more days before I can really get anything to you."

"Oh," I said, with more disappointment than I intended. Surely, I couldn't expect to be Preston's main focus. Of course he had other jobs he was seeing to. Then I heard my phone beep and when I pulled it away, I saw a text message from Derrek. "Can you hold on one second, Preston? I just got a text."

"Sure."

I pulled the phone away from my ear again and activated the screen.

We're going to a Gala tomorrow night. One of the charities the company supports is throwing a fundraiser. Formal. I'll be there at seven to pick you up.

"Shit," I said as I finished reading it. I put the phone back up to my ear just as Preston started speaking.

"Lena? Is everything all right?"

I sighed. "No, not really. Derrek says we have to go to a fundraiser tomorrow night. I hate those enough to begin with, but having to pretend to be his happy wife for an evening really doesn't sound like my idea of a fun time." I rubbed the little bundle of wrinkles between my eyebrows, the skin bunching there from the tension rolling through my body.

Preston was silent at the other end of the line, but the silence also allowed me to hear his car turning off, signaling he'd arrived wherever he was headed.

"Anyway, sorry to bother you. Take your time with the case. I'm just anxious to get out of here."

"Lena," he whispered my name like it hurt him to do so. His voice was pained and thick, soft but strained. "Don't go."

"What?" My reply was whispered, just like his voice.

"Don't go. Don't. Make up some excuse, but don't go with him."

My mouth opened to say something, but then closed again, my mind not coming up with a reply.

"Preston, I have to go. I'm his wife," I finally uttered. I heard him inhale and I winced, feeling like I'd hurt him somehow with my words.

"You're only his wife on paper," he said, sounding angrier, harsher.

"That's the only part that matters right now."

"His money can't be so important to you that you'd basically sell yourself. That's what you're doing, Lena. You're selling yourself if you go with him. You're pretending to be his wife for money. What does that make you?"

Now it was my turn to be angry. "What, exactly, are you trying to say?" I turned out of the living room, headed to my bedroom and walked to my window, pulling the curtains back just slightly. Just enough to see his black Lotus in its usual spot a few houses down.

"I don't want you with him." This statement was spoken in a voice still firm and a little angry, but also pleading.

His words evoked so many emotions from me it was hard to nail one down. The overwhelming feelings were happiness and warmth. Preston cared enough about me to want to keep me from Derrek. Whether this was out of just macho dominance or genuine concern, it didn't matter. It'd been years since someone cared about me and I wanted to wrap myself up in it. But all of that happiness was tamped down by my need to get out of my marriage intact. I couldn't let my emotions ruin my plans.

"Preston, I don't want to be with him, either," I said as I looked at his car. I strained to see his form through the windows, but he was too far. The urge to lay my eyes on him was overwhelming. Just to see him. That was all I needed. "Will you do me a favor?" I whispered.

"Anything," he replied, making my eyes close and the breath steal away from me.

"Can you get out of your car for just a moment?"

He didn't answer, just opened his car door and got out, walking to the front of it, staring right at me in my bedroom window. I bit down on my lips to keep myself from asking him to come in, because I knew, without a doubt, if I invited him in the game would be over.

"You're always gone when I wake up. How long do you stay out there?"

"Until I know for sure you're safe." His answer was both infuriating and beautiful.

"Goodnight, Preston."

"Sleep tight, sweetheart."

The next night, I found myself wasting a fantastic dress on Derrek. I turned in the mirror to check the back of the dress. Yup. What a waste.

From the waist up, the dress was all black lace. It had a tight collar neck with capped sleeves. The lace came down the back, but in the front there was a rather large keyhole. It was big enough to show decent cleavage, but not distastefully. The lace went down to my hips where it met a soft, pink flowing material that floated out around me whenever I moved, swishing in a way that made most girls smile. It was the kind of material that made you want to move to see and feel the fabric swirl around you. It had a high-low hem, so the front came to just above my knees, but the back floated all the way to the ground. The lace was used in the bottom half of the dress as detail, and swirled daintily around my hips and curves.

My dark hair was up in a sophisticated twist with a few tendrils left down to curl around my face. My makeup was soft and natural. The only jewelry I wore were the diamond solitaire earrings my father gave me for college graduation and my wedding ring.

I heard the front door open and took a deep breath in, trying to ready myself to spend an evening pretending to be happy with my husband. I heard him walking toward the bedroom and my eyes moved to the door. He walked briskly through the door, glancing at me, then moving back toward the dresser, where he stopped and opened the top drawer. I noticed he was in a tuxedo and I wondered, briefly, where he'd gotten ready. Then I laughed softly because I realized exactly where he'd dressed. I also noticed he spared not even three seconds to admire me in this dress, in which I looked fantastic. But just as quickly as his eyes passed over me, the thought flitted from my mind. I didn't need or want him to desire me. I wanted out. Unfortunately, I was forced to spend the next few hours with him.

"Are you ready to go?" he asked as he put new cufflinks in.

"Yup," I said, popping the P at the end of the word.

"Great, the town car is outside waiting for you."

I wasted no time walking outside, only stopping to grab my coat. As I walked down the path to the waiting car, I saw the black Lotus drive slowly past my house and my heart rate spiked, knowing Preston was inside the car. The car continued down the road, turning at the corner, and then disappearing. I took in a sharp breath when I heard the front door close behind me and heard Derrek's voice.

"Lena, we don't have all night. Let's go." He was being impatient. Fantastic. I climbed in the car, hoping Preston didn't follow us. I didn't need this kind of drama tonight. I just wanted to get the event over with and go home, hopefully without Derrek, and hopefully with Preston in his car down the road. It was selfish of me, I realized, but I also didn't care. What I didn't need was Preston making a scene. I hoped he was smart enough to realize that and keep his distance.

An hour later, we were fully surrounded by Derrek's co-workers and employees. There were many other people in attendance and occasionally Derrek would pull me away to meet people he was trying to network with. I played my part: smiled, nodded, and pretended to be interested in their conversation. I also withheld from shooting glares at Derrek when his hand rested on the small of my back, or he leaned over and placed soft kisses on my neck behind my ear. In the past, these gestures would have left me swooning, my heartbeat pulsing through my veins, my need for him building, the anticipation of our night in bed filling my mind. Instead, I tried not to roll my eyes when he touched me. At one point, I found myself fantasizing about Preston kicking my door down and rushing to find me in bed, waiting for him, naked.

I was pulled from my daydream, and caught completely off guard, when Derrek interrupted me with an introduction that sounded forced and uncomfortable.

"Ms. Fahey, this is my wife, Lena."

I turned to see the woman I was being introduced to was, in fact, my husband's mistress. I deserved an academy award for my performance over the next few minutes. Not only was I able to keep my face from showing any of the discomfort I was feeling as I eyed the woman sleeping with my husband, but I managed to ignore the glare she was not as good at hiding from me. She looked me up and down, obviously sizing up the competition.

"Lena, this is Jessica Fahey. She's the assistant to the CEO." I smiled sweetly at her, secretly pleased that I was already winning the 'Who Can Keep Their Cool' competition. She was losing, miserably.

"It's so nice to meet you," I said, with a smile. "I love your dress." Her dress was hideous.

She tilted her head to the side and tried to smile, but it came off sort of like a grimace. "Thanks. Your wedding ring is lovely," she said, gesturing to my hand.

No way that bitch was gutsy enough to gawk at my wedding ring. She obviously had no idea I knew who she was, or that she was fucking my husband. I played right along, though.

"Oh, thanks," I cried, holding my hand out for her to examine the ring. "It's three carats," I said, sighing, playing up the smitten wife role. I leaned into her and whispered, "Do you want to try it on? I don't mind." She pulled back from me like she'd been bitten. *Oh, I think I touched a nerve.* She looked as if she tasted something sour and then she took a stance as if to lunge at me, but Derrek grabbed her elbow and strode her away from me, saying something about having to discuss a certain account with her.

As he ushered her away from me, I felt a strange sensation, as if I were being watched. The hairs on the back of my neck stood up and my heart pounded in my chest. My head swiveled to the left, then to the right, but I saw nothing out of the ordinary. My eyes found Derrek again and I watched as he tried to calm Jessica down, tried to keep her from causing a scene. She looked near tears and it was obvious my being there was distressing to her. *Join the club, lady.* I couldn't watch my husband comfort his mistress any longer, so I turned to find the restroom.

I walked down the hallway along the far end of the ballroom, guessing I would find the restrooms somewhere close by. My heels were clacking on the hard floors, a sound I had always enjoyed hearing, and I focused on the echo it made. Then, the echo of my shoes was joined by the sound of another set of shoes walking behind me. Before I could process the extra footfalls, I felt a hand on my elbow and I was being pulled through a door to my right.

I was tugged into the room and I stumbled a few steps, trying to regain my balance. The room was lit, but dimly, and all I could focus on was Preston and his face, which looked like a cross between pained and furious.

"What are you doing here?" I asked, my voice urgent but quiet. I did not need to be discovered in a utility closet with a man who wasn't my husband. "And what is your problem? You can't just yank me around!"

"I didn't *yank* you." He was pacing around the room like a caged tiger. As he walked back and forth, he ran his hand through his hair, and I couldn't help but notice he was wearing a tuxedo. This was not a tuxedo he'd rented for an evening. This was *his* tuxedo, and it was tailored specifically for him. Even though most of his body was covered, I'd never been so enraptured by it before. The man wore that tuxedo in a way that made my entire body want to crawl inside of it with him.

"Preston, why are you here?"

"He had his hands on you." He stopped pacing when he spoke, looking directly at me. I swallowed hard, taking in the sharp features of his face, made even more striking by his anger. He took a step toward me and I instinctively took a step backward. He continued in my direction and I retreated until I was pressed against a wall, and he was just feet away. I had nowhere to go so I just tipped my chin up and looked him in the eye, not backing down. "I would have stayed out of sight," he said, stopping inches from me. "I planned to stay out of sight, but then he had to put his hands on you."

I took a deep breath in, but he was so close my breasts pushed against him. I exhaled quickly, enjoying the contact too much, and then tried to respond to him.

"He's my husband," I managed, if only a strangled whisper, his face now just a breath away from mine.

"But you belong to me." I didn't have time to respond to his words before his mouth crashed down onto mine. I fought his mouth, my hands coming to his chest to push him away at first, but then his tongue slid along the seam of my lips, and when I moaned involuntarily, he snuck in. My body couldn't fight him anymore, didn't want to fight him. My mind was quickly ticking through all the reasons kissing Preston was the worst mistake I could make in that moment, but rather quickly, as his hands began to slide up my sides, barely brushing the edge of my breasts, the reasons I shouldn't kiss him morphed into the reasons I never wanted to stop.

When he felt me give in to him, something else inside him snapped, and the kiss went even deeper. His tongue swiped through my mouth and my tongue was desperate to find his. His hands found the sides of my face, angling me perfectly to take even more from me.

Good God.

The man could kiss.

My hands slid up the front of him, running into the buttons of his tux jacket. I undid the buttons and pushed his coat aside, only to encounter the vest, which I hastily unbuttoned as well. Finally, only the thin layer of his dress shirt was between my hands and his chest and I could feel every ripple of muscle the man was hiding. Muscles I'd been imagining every day since I first met him in that bar. I clutched his shirt, my back arching, trying to get as close to him as possible.

As he kissed me, he unleashed a growl and my reaction was instinct. I moaned as wetness pooled between my legs and my hands shook with anticipation. His left hand moved to the back of my neck, keeping my mouth pressed firmly against his, while his right hand slid down my front, over my breast. His hand cupped my lace-covered breast, his thumb pressing gently over my nipple, so hard he could no doubt feel it through my dress.

I moaned again, louder this time, causing our mouths to break apart. My eyes closed and my head rolled back, unable to focus on anything besides sensation. His thumb and forefinger tugged on my nipple through my dress and I mewled again, my clit pulsing, begging for contact. I felt his mouth between my breasts, licking the valley there, as his hand moved lower.

"Preston," I moaned. I knew we shouldn't continue, knew I should push him away, but the rational part of my brain was being held hostage by the part that wanted to fuck him in this room. Wanted to feel him inside of me, wanted all of him, and there was no reasoning with this part. I didn't even try.

"Be quiet, sweetheart," he whispered, the anger gone from his voice. He sounded softer but still gruff. He sounded like he was aroused, and hearing his voice like that, calling me sweetheart, catapulted me into another stratosphere. His mouth left my cleavage and I felt him move lower, my eyes moving to watch him crouch to the ground. As he slid down, his hands grazed down the sides of me, leaving trails of electricity and sparks behind. Everywhere he touched me turned to fire.

When his face aligned with the part of me pulsing and throbbing, I silently begged him to put his mouth on me. I wanted nothing more in that moment than to feel his tongue slide through me. Instead, his eyes moved back to mine and he spoke.

"In another place, in another time, I'd bury my face in you so fast, my only goal to make you scream my name. But not tonight, Lena." With those breathtaking words, his hands softly started at my knees and then moved to the back of my thighs, sliding up and over my ass, then stopped at the top of my panties. I gasped when he pulled them gently down my legs, stopping at my ankles. "Lift."

Without giving it much thought, I raised one foot, watching him carefully maneuver the lacy, beige thong around the high heels, then he gently tapped my other ankle and we repeated the process. He stood slowly, my panties in his hand, and gave me a sexy, sultry smile. I was still lightly panting, my body not used to being this revved up. Then my breath stopped completely when he placed my panties in the front breast pocket of his tuxedo jacket.

"Now these belong to me, too."

"Preston," I started, only to be stopped again by his mouth. With his lips pressed firmly against mine, his hands brushed up the outside of my thighs, bringing my dress up with them until I was bare from the waist down. His left arm wrapped around my waist, holding up my dress and his other hand found its way to my ass, palming it, pulling me closer to him.

I was bare, being pushed against his front, and all I could feel was his erection pressing into me. Without much thought to anything else besides the heat between my legs, I wrapped one leg around his hip, allowing the very center of me to press up against him.

His fingers moved softly over the swell of my ass, over the crease between my hip and thigh, and continued down the front of me until his fingers were teasing the very spot that ached for him. He continued to kiss me as his fingers gently parted me and slowly dipped in, seeming to test me. I reached down between us, my hand covering his wrist, urging him on, hoping he'd give me what I needed.

"Please," I breathed against his kiss, and I cried out as his fingers pushed farther into me. Our foreheads pressed together as we both looked down to see his hand working in and out of me.

"Christ, you're wet," he growled.

With each swipe of his fingers, I felt him graze that spot buried deep inside me that triggered me to gasp and shake all over. He felt it, too, fed off my reaction to his touch, and every time his fingers delved into me, he was searching for that perfect spot.

His forehead pulled away from mine and his lips wandered to my neck, just adding to the pile of sensations I would have to walk away from when it was all over. His tongue on my skin, his breath on my ear, his fingers gently, but firmly, fucking me into bliss – all of it, I would have to leave behind. Any depressing thoughts of Preston's hands never being on me again were promptly shoved to the side when his fingers landed directly on the perfect spot, a place deep inside that, truly, I'd been the only one to find in the past. His teeth nipping at my neck, his arm around my waist, and his fore and middle fingers working me over; all those caused my head to tip back and a stifled cry to leave me. As if that weren't enough, his thumb then found my clit, a power-move I was sure he was saving until that very moment to send me over the edge. His thumb circled it feverishly and I simply crackled. Sizzled. I was aflame. I thrust my pelvis into his hand, wanting everything he could give me, taking everything he was offering, and I might have climbed up him as I came.

The orgasm he gave me went on and on, and perhaps was more than one, but I couldn't tell. I was floating on a cloud, having the best out-of-body experience I could imagine. When I felt myself finally flutter back to the ground, with Preston's fingers still gingerly stroking me, my eyes came back into focus and I looked at him. Before I could get a word out, his lips came to mine again, but this time, the kiss was sweet and slow.

His left hand found its way back to my face, cupping my cheek, and his other hand wrapped around my waist, simply holding me to him. I tightened my leg around him, still needing to be as close to him as possible, knowing he was going to pull away eventually and I'd have to give him up forever.

When he did tear his lips from mine, it was only far enough away to say my name against them.

"Lena," he whispered. "I'm sorry." His words we pained but his touch was still soft. "I didn't want this to happen here."

"It's a little late for regrets," I said, letting my leg drop back to the ground.

"No," he said, gripping me behind my knee and pulling my leg back to his hip. "I could never regret touching you. I just regret doing it here. I wanted you in my bed, Lena. I want you naked, lying down, completely bare and spread for me. Open for me to see and feel. I want every piece of you, and I want to be able to make you scream my name without worry of who might hear. I didn't want to fuck you with my hand in a broom closet."

"Then why did you?"

"He had his hands on you," he repeated his words from earlier.

"He's my husband." I repeated mine.

"I don't care what some stupid piece of paper says, Lena. You've been mine since the very first time I saw you walk into that bar."

My eyebrows scrunched at his words. "You couldn't have watched me walk into the bar. I beat you there. I watched *you* come in."

His thumb came up and traced over my bottom lip. "Will you always underestimate me?" He said the words with a smile, but I felt the word 'always' like it hit me in the gut. We wouldn't have an always. We had a 'right this instant,' and it was closely followed with a 'this is so terribly wrong.' I couldn't help but feel like it was the best wrong I'd ever had.

"I beat you there by about twenty minutes, but I was waiting outside. As I watched you walk in to that bar, I knew everything in my world was about to be flipped upside down, and I followed you in anticipation of that."

"Preston," I said softly. "This," I said, using my hand to motion between us, "It doesn't change anything." I took in a breath, hoping the words didn't hurt as much coming out as it did holding them in. "When I walk out of here, we can't be together again. It's too dangerous. I can't even believe I let this happen, here, with Derrek just in another room." I put my hands back on his chest, trying to push him away again, but his hands were firmly planted on my thigh and waist, and he wasn't letting go. "I need to deal with my marriage. I need to put that behind me before I can even start to think about being with someone else."

My leg fell back down as his hand moved from my thigh to cup the side of my face, then moved just slightly into the hair pinned back, pulling me closer to him.

"You need to let me worry about Derrek. I'll get what you need. But you can't push me away, sweetheart. You've already let me partway in, and I plan on getting all the way in soon. In every sense of the word."

"What if I don't want you in at all?" I tried to use a voice more forceful and strong, but I was sure I sounded shaky and unsure.

He pressed me up against the wall again and I could feel his cock, rock hard still, between us. I whimpered involuntarily, unprepared to feel him hard and huge against me, and as he leaned down and nipped my bottom lip between his teeth, he ground his hips into me, my traitorous eyes fluttering closed.

"You're a shit liar, Lena. You're dripping for me right now." Even as he said the words, his hand ran over my opening, making me cry out, a sound of pleasure mixed with surprise. He pushed his fingers into me again, slowly, and I couldn't hold back my moan as I exhaled. "Here's what you're going to do." His fingers slid out of me and my eyes snapped open, looking to him for explanation. "You're going to walk out of here," his fingers pushed back in, making my mouth gape open. Then he pulled out and made a slow circle around my clit, eliciting more cries from me. "You're going to walk right out of this gala." He lazily slipped his fingers back in and then out again. "You're going to get a cab home and then wait for me." The warmth of his hand was then absent altogether, and I hated that I missed it.

"You're going to fuck everything up," I said, accepting the fact I wasn't in control anymore, and that even though Preston was, the odds were against me.

"Hardly, sweetheart. I'm going to fuck *you*. But it's not going to be in a closet, and it's not going to be fast or quick. I'm going to fuck you in my bed, slow and hard, and then I'm going to do it again and again until we're both exhausted and sore in all the good places."

I swallowed hard, both completely aroused by his promises, and scared about the reality that waited for me outside this utility closet.

"I can't just leave. Derrek will wonder where I've gone. We're supposed to be putting on a show for everyone, parading our happy marriage for all to see."

"I'll take care of Derrek." My eyebrows rose in doubt. "Trust me," he said, reading me.

"Okay," I whispered.

"Good girl," he said against my lips, before he took them again in a scorching kiss. It was wet and hot and long. It was also full of promises – vows made directly to my body, which I instantly and stupidly believed.

He pulled away from the kiss, his hands trailing down my neck, and he said, "Go now, sweetheart. I'll meet you at your house."

For reasons I couldn't quite understand, I did exactly as he asked. I left the utility closet and walked straight out of the gala, not speaking to anyone except the clerk working the coat check when I retrieved my coat and purse. I walked out of the building, hailed a cab, and rode home. All the while, I was painfully aware I had no panties on.

For most of the ride, my mind flipped and flopped from thinking about how stupid I was being for even entertaining the idea of getting involved with Preston, to then picturing his hand as it thrust inside me, making me come inside a closet. By the time the cab pulled up in front of my house, I had really only come to one conclusion.

I wanted Preston inside me. Desperately. All of him.

So I walked inside to prepare to give myself to someone other than my husband. I had everything to lose and practically nothing to gain, but I couldn't bring myself to care.

END OF PART ONE

Make sure you look for Part Two, Private Encounters, coming soon!

Acknowledgements

First I want to thank every author whose serials I have read and enjoyed. I found a little pocket of literature that I really am drawn to, and was inspired because of it. I know serials aren't everyone's favorite reads, but I find them challenging in a completely different way and loved the way this particular story allowed me to spread my wings.

To the readers, thank you for taking a chance on this new adventure. I hope Lena and Preston kept you on the edge of your seat and that you are looking forward to Private Encounters. To my readers who have followed me throughout my short, yet exciting, career – THANK YOU for reading this project. I love you for having faith in me and my work. To the new readers, WELCOME! I am so glad you are here!

To my family, thank you for all your usual support.

To the ladies at Hot Tree Editing, thank you for making this project so fun and for making it the best it could be.

To all the blogs who signed up to help with my surprise release, I thank you so much. I am forever grateful for your support.

To Becca, Andrea, Lesley, and Kelly, thank you all for reading this story and providing me with invaluable feedback. I appreciate you all so much.

Please feel free to follow me on any and all media platforms!

http://www.facebook.com/AuthorAnieMichaels

https://twitter.com/Anie_Michaels

Shoot me an email!

anie.michaels@gmail.com

Sign up for my newsletter to stay up to date on exciting news and new releases!

http://eepurl.com/-DPjn